P9-EDW-600

WITHDRAWN
UTSA LIBRARIES

Nectar at Noon

BY SHEILA CUDAHY

Poems   1962
Clod's Calvary & other poems   1972
The Bristle Cone Pine & other poems   1976
translation of *No Way* by Natalia Ginzburg   1974
The Trojan Gold   1979

Nectar at Noon

STORIES BY

Sheila Cudahy

HARCOURT BRACE JOVANOVICH, PUBLISHERS

SAN DIEGO   NEW YORK   LONDON

HBJ

Copyright © 1989 by Sheila Cudahy Pellegrini

All rights reserved.
No part of this publication may be reproduced
or transmitted in any form or by any means,
electronic or mechanical, including photocopy,
recording, or any information storage and retrieval
system, without permission in writing
from the publisher.

Requests for permission to make copies of any
part of the work should be mailed to:
Copyrights and Permissions Department,
Harcourt Brace Jovanovich, Publishers,
Orlando, Florida 32887.

Library of Congress Cataloging-in-Publication Data
Cudahy, Sheila.
    Nectar at noon: stories/by Sheila Cudahy. — 1st ed.
    p.   cm.
    ISBN 0-15-152170-0
    I. Title.
    PS3553.U27L68   1989
    813'.54 — dc19   89-30821

Designed by Ann Gold
Printed in the United States of America
First edition
A B C D E

Library
University of Texas
at San Antonio

Contents

Illuminations

I AM GIVEN TO moments of enlightenment. An instantaneous grasp of the entire IRS code, a vision of the cosmos to the tenth dimension in which time and space are braided with light. These and lesser truths, such as the fact that the sparrow outside the window chides her young in French, "Taisez-vous, taisez-vous," come to me in the early morning while I am lying, eyes closed, but awake and content, in the warmth of my body and Eliot's next to me.

I do not share them. My old friend and professor, Dr. Gustav Muller, the distinguished mathematician, warned me against doing so. One day he presented several of his graduate students with a complicated equation. When to my surprise I saw the solution immediately and blurted it out, disrupting the class, he took me aside and said, "You have intuition, yes. It is a gift the Bible calls prophecy, the theologians grace. But in my view, it is merely the intellect at play." In his youth Muller had studied the Bible, put God on trial and found Him to be a non-being. Nevertheless, he enjoyed quoting Scripture to make a point. "Remember, truth, like the wind, bloweth where it listeth."

On those occasions when it bloweth my way, I lie quietly and say nothing, but this morning's revelation is so compelling that I whisper, "Eliot, I possess the proof for the existence of God."

A cheek, cool and scented with after-shave lotion, brushes mine. "It's late. Tell me at lunch, love."

I call after him that what I have to tell him can't wait until noon, but he is out the door.

"Dépêchez-vous, dépêchez-vous," mother sparrow commands, and I hurry to my fourth graders.

The misery of arithmetic is evident in their faces. Flu, measles, the maladies of spring have reduced their numbers. The survivors watch listlessly as I pass among them handing out the work books. Johnny Rader coughs into his hands. A blue vein like a scar threads Crissie Stone's right temple and disappears at the dark hair line. As I proceed to the front of the room, I hear a scuffle. Books fall to the floor directly behind me. That will be Tom Hall deliberately dropping his and knocking down Sara Cowles's as well. Tom is always testing me. He knows I'm new because he had a different teacher last year, one who didn't pass him. Now forced to repeat, he is the biggest and oldest in the class and vents his boredom and frustration on me and timid little Sara. Fortunately he doesn't know how inexperienced I am. A Ph.D. in mathematics is a joke compared with attempting to hold the attention of a not-too-bright bully, but I am determined he's not going to fail again. From my desk I face the class. The children droop in the close air, their small boneless faces pallid under the strip lighting.

"Who remembers what we learned yesterday?" No one remembers. They are adrift, beyond reach. "Sets, class, we learned about sets of numbers." They stare with the empty eyes of the drowned. I struggle to revive them. "Number, children. The beauty of number." Turning my back on them, I draw a huge circle on the blackboard. The chalk squeaks horribly. "Oweee," I hear Crissie squeal as I continue: "Here is the universe and everything in it, everything and everyone you can think of. Use your imagination. It's like a bird caged in your head. Let it fly and carry you." All is quiet behind me. I add tiny circles inside the whole. "Here is Mary and John and Sara." I write names next to each circle, including those of the absent. A stir of bodies fills the room, and glancing over my shoulder I see rows of faces uplifted and floating toward me. Elated, I grab a piece of yellow chalk and sketch stars, comets, nebulae. "Each one of us has a secret number, and like the heavenly bodies we spin around a motionless center." I place a wet forefinger in the middle of the circle. The spot quickly dries to a faint smudge. "You can't see this point with your eyes. It's too bright, the most brilliant number of all, but you can see it with your minds, and sometimes, especially at night, you can hear the music of the stars as they whirl and play." My throat is parched. My head aches from the effort to simplify my vision for the children. I have much more to tell them: how the universe is infused with energy, how for the energy pulsing in each particle there is a harmony, an order. They must grasp that point. "Harmony, order, children." I turn to

3

the class. The room is empty. The recess bell fades in the din of feet scuffling in the corridor.

From the classroom window I can see the playground. The fence around the asphalt compound seems barely sufficient to contain the teeming chaos of small bodies as they ricochet off one another. Some gang together and clash, one cluster against another, then they break loose and scatter, tumbling, kicking, punching at random.

Agnes Scott, a thin and alert jogger, patrols the perimeter. New teachers get playground duty. My turn comes next week, and I am struck by her terrified expression as she watches for the moment when roughhousing explodes into savagery: the fist clenching a rock, the stomping boot. Some of my fourth graders are out of harm's way on the jungle gym. I spot Tom Hall in hot pursuit of a sturdy blonde from the fifth grade. She zigs and zags, keeping just ahead, then halts suddenly and faces him. Other girls close around her, giggling and pointing. Tom backs away and bumps into Sara, who is playing hopscotch by herself. In a fury he grabs her knitted cap and throws it on top of the fence out of reach. Agnes races to the rescue. I hate Tom Hall. I have tried all year not to let him fail, but he's winning. Crissie, I see no sign of her. She and Sara are best friends. Where is she? The school insists that the teachers require every child to play unless excused. I hurry downstairs, and as I approach the door leading to the playground, I see Crissie hunched over on the floor, her arms wrapped around her bare legs. A bruise, or maybe it's just grime, darkens her right cheekbone. As I reach down to comfort her, the bell rings. She jumps up sobbing and scurries up the stairs ahead of the onrush of bodies.

"Thank God it's Friday," Agnes calls to me as together

we attempt to make the children form an orderly line. "Walk, not run, please. No shoving. I mean you, Tom." Agnes and I follow into the building.

"I'm afraid Crissie may have a shiner," Agnes tells me. "Nothing serious. She started the fight and got the worst of it. The little darlings are all yours next week."

JACK'S CHOP HOUSE is already crowded when I arrive. A dark tunnel of a place, it serves a moderately-priced businessman's lunch from the bar and in booths along one wall. I edge my way along the barrier of dark blue suits at the bar where backs are being slapped, loud laughter triggering louder laughter. "Hi, Jennie," Jack shouts and waves me to the last empty booth. Eliot must be giving him free advice on his divorce. "Where's the legal eagle?" He hovers in the dim light of a fake carriage lamp.

"He's coming."

A busboy carrying a tray of dirty dishes clatters between us. I gaze absently across the room. A large green-tinted mirror behind the bar reflects the collared, cravatted fronts of the slapped backs. Mouths, jowls, throats, gulping like frogs, animate the fronts. I wish some avenging angel would crash through the glass and put all the frogs to the sword. I wish Eliot would come. Friday is my *only* free lunch hour away from school. I wish I could forget my fourth graders, especially Tom Hall.

A waiter with a blackboard noting the day's specials comes over. He's losing money on this booth.

"My husband will be here any minute." I order a beer out of guilt.

Eliot is eighteen minutes late. I realize young lawyers in big firms get dumped on. It's part of the system, like playground duty, but he is later than usual. Mugged, run over, a heart attack at twenty-nine? Maybe he's been fired and is cleaning out his desk. We'll move to Montana and live in a cabin on tofu and vegetables.

"Sorry, love." He slides in beside me, and for a moment we sit like two animals warming each other.

"We ought to order right away. The waiter was here, now he's disappeared."

"Relax. He'll come."

He does, I order the vegetable soup, Eliot the pork chops.

"You look beat. The class go okay?" He scrutinizes my face.

"Yes, I guess it did, but maybe I'm not meant to be a teacher. I'd like to do something that makes a difference."

"With your qualifications IBM would hire you in a shot, at three times the salary."

"I'm not sure I want to work for a big corporation."

"After a morning like this one at Hawkins Collins Freund, I see your point. It's like answering to God or Satan. I'm not sure which. Maybe both." He laughs and muses, "God Hawkins and Devil Collins. What did you want to tell me this morning?"

"This morning? Seems ages ago."

"You were still in bed. I hated to rush away." He takes my hand.

Seeing his moony smile I say quickly, "It wasn't that. I just saw something."

"What?"

The waiter slides the plates onto the table, giving me

the pork chops. Eliot rearranges the dishes. I watch the soup swirl to the rim of the bowl and settle.

"Everything okay?" Jack elbows his way past the booth without stopping.

"What was it you were going to tell me?"

I grip Eliot's hand as he starts to pick up his knife. "Something beautiful like an enormous mobile with a goose neck or one of those oil pumps that seesaw, only floating in the air, at times like a baby elephant in profile, all ears and swinging its trunk."

"What was it really?" He looks at his watch, and I release my grip of his hand.

"Nothing you can touch. More like chords."

"Chords?"

"Musical chords progressing up and down, only without sound."

Eliot catches the waiter's eye and pantomime-scribbles in the air for the check. "I'm listening."

The proof of the existence of God drifts like a crippled kite in the vaulted darkness. The more I try to reel it in, the more it veers crashing against the mirror, and then, sucked by the currents of the ceiling fans, it circles erratically.

"I'm sorry I can't tell you. I lost it on the playground."

"You've lost me, love."

"The children, they're so cruel to each other, so unreachable." I turn away from him and through a brief blur of tears see a new crowd of latecomers arrive at the bar.

"Isn't the soup all right?" the waiter is asking me, removing it.

"I'm not hungry. Just coffee."

"Next Friday we'll go someplace else and take as long

as we want. To hell with Cromwell versus Wells. I want to talk to my wife."

"How about a tent in Maine?"

"Wouldn't that be great?" He sighs, already there, and snuggles against me. "You know, this morning I figured maybe you were going to tell me you were pregnant. Are you?"

"No, thank God."

"But you like kids. I thought that's why you went into teaching." He takes the check from the waiter.

"There's a kite on the ceiling. It looks like a bat."

"Sure, love, or a baby elephant in profile. Let's go. Tonight we'll take the phone off the hook. I want to tell you about a sex discrimination case I'm working on."

BACK IN THE CLASSROOM I find the fourth grade flushed, edgy with unspent energy. While I am taking attendance, I sense a presence in the doorway. It is Miss Wells, the veteran homeroom teacher come to take over. Eyes follow her as she strides to the desk where I am hurriedly gathering up my books.

"Interesting." Miss Wells adjusts her rimless glasses and surveys the blackboard.

"That's the universe." Tom Hall stands up boldly. "And in the center is," he hesitates and looks lost. "Well, you can't see it, but I'm right over there." He points a grubby finger.

Instantly hands shoot up pleading for equal time. Miss Wells ignores them and eyes me. I realize I have sinned. The school requires every teacher to leave the blackboard clean.

"Sorry, Miss Wells, I forgot." I am shocked to hear

myself sounding exactly like a fourth grader. Next I'll be saying, "If you're nice to me I'll be your best friend." I drop my things on the desk and grab an eraser.

"Christina, come up and help Mrs. Harper so we can get on with social studies," Miss Wells orders.

I start wiping out the top of the universe, leaving the bottom for Crissie.

"What's the matter with your face?" Miss Wells peers at Crissie's bruise. "Here's a tissue."

"It's not dirt, Miss Wells," Crissie answers sullenly, watching me destroy Halley's comet.

The celestial order disappears in puffs of chalk dust. One by one the little circles fade under my eraser. Crissie flinches when I obliterate her name.

"Thank you, Mrs. Harper," Miss Wells says. "Return to your seat, Christina. Come to the board, Tom."

To make certain that I have overlooked nothing, I stand back from the cosmos. The faint smudge in the center remains. I leave it. Tom sees it and gives me a conspiratorial smile. I smile back and rush from the room.

Towing

I'M STEAMING but I can't tell Velma, my smart-ass step-mother, that Bruce and I have just had the worst fight of our relationship, worse even than last fall, the day we met when some jerk in the school cafeteria line started shoving and suddenly Bruce and I were jammed against each other over cheeseburgers floating in V-8.

"Love at first fight," Velma says whenever Bruce's name is mentioned, and it has been mentioned a lot this summer.

"Where's Bruce?" she asks the minute I walk in the door. Saturday is her house plant day, and she is dabbing the leaves of a philodendron in the kitchen sink.

"With the Barracuda at the car wash."

"He certainly loves that car."

I can't deny it. This summer has been a real drag. During the day Bruce spends all his time customizing the Barracuda, and at night he has nothing but cruising and sex on his mind. Big thrill, cruising Route 25 through Perrytown, the deadest town in the middle of Maryland. He thinks Maryland is the greatest, although he only moved here last fall. He has lived everywhere, on account of the company his father works for transferring the family all over the country.

The argument today started about the Baltimore Orioles, and then being Saturday it was groom the Barracuda time. Every Saturday we spend hours at Jerry's Automatic Car Wash. First we park by the heavy-duty vacuum. My job is to clean the upholstery—red velvet, simulated—while Bruce polishes the dash and miles of chrome trim on the body. He began giving me a hard time the minute I turned on the vac. "There's gravel under the back seat. And don't forget the carpeting in the trunk." The roof of the Barracuda is black vinyl, and in the sun the stupid car turns into a microwave. I was so hot and sweaty I almost looked forward to the car wash tunnel. Almost but not really. The tunnel, the torrents of water and those gigantic brushes whirling out of the darkness around the car scare me. When the windows fog over and the Barracuda begins to vibrate I feel as if we were airborne in a storm. Bruce considers the automatic car wash one of life's great erotic experiences, but at the thought of him and me kissing forever in that tunnel I freeze. Today I froze and exploded. At the entrance Bruce slammed on the brakes. "How come you forgot to vac the seat belts?"

Vac the seat belts! I can't remember what I said when I jumped out, but it made him so furious he forgot to close his window. As the flood engulfed the hood I could hear him shouting "Wah wah wah." Bruce's blond head and the "I ♥ Maryland" bumper sticker disappeared in the foam and I walked home.

"You two have had one of your fights." Velma turns her X-ray eyes on me.

She's a psychologist, does a lot of counseling, so I sure as hell don't want to tell her what happened. She gives up the eye contact and shakes the plant over the sink. "I just wonder when you're going to get off the emotional roller coaster that boy has got you on and take control of your life."

To stop the rest of Velma's lecture I say I'm going to clean out my closets. She immediately hands me a box of Hefties—trash can size—and speeds me on my way to becoming a real person with promises of iced tea as soon as she has exterminated the aphids. In my room I watch an old Bugs Bunny cartoon on TV without the sound so I can hear the phone the minute Bruce calls. Our rule is that whoever starts the fight apologizes first thing. While Bugs booby-traps Doc's wheelbarrow I attack my bureau drawers.

Under the sox is a small stack of snapshots. Every Christmas my mother, who lives with my stepfather Ralph on the Eastern Shore, sends me a colored photo of herself, Ralph, and his children, Sherrylee and Ralph Jr. The picture is always the same. The kids, who have washed-out faces under the freckles, stand between my mother and Ralph on a tiny strip of yellow sand. They look like cutouts pasted on a fake sky. No Christmas tree, no Chesapeake Bay. Nothing. One year a little black dog appeared in Sherrylee's arms, but by the next Christmas card he had vanished. From then on it's just been the four of them clutching one another as if they were afraid of being blown out of the picture. Before each vacation my mother phones asking me to visit them so

I can get to know the kids, who live with their mother in Baltimore except on holidays. My mother sounds disappointed when I make excuses for not coming, but I'm afraid if I went, I'd be the one to disappear.

Doc's wheelbarrow is exploding as I toss the photos in a Hefty. The phone rings in the kitchen. I dash for the stairs but Velma has already answered and is speaking in her professional healer's voice. These conversations with her clients can last forever. Bruce is probably in a phone booth trying to reach me. However, Velma hangs up in less than a minute. On the TV Hepburn is hurling golf clubs at Cary Grant. I stay awake until they make up. It occurs to me that Bruce isn't playing by the rules.

In the morning Velma says, "Nice if you would join us." Every Sunday she and my father visit her parents, whom she insists on calling my grandparents, which they aren't. All my grandparents are dead. "It's Grandfather's birthday."

I know I can't handle that, but I've got to get out of the house or I'll go crazy waiting for the phone, so on the way I ask my father to drop me off at Uncle Willard's. He isn't really my uncle, just a distant relative of one of my dead grandparents, but I've known him all my life. My father used to take his second-hand Buick Riviera for repairs to Willard's Gas Station and Wrecker Service on Route 25, until Velma convinced him that Uncle Willard drank too much.

"Say hello for us," Velma calls as they drive away.

Although the sign on the glass door says COME IN, WE'RE OPEN, there is no one in the office, so I walk around to the back of the building. Uncle Willard is seated on a bench under a lean-to he and his son Buddy built. The roof is corrugated green plastic that turns the sunlight and Uncle Willard's cap—mesh crown and

Amoco label on the peak—a bright emerald. He is staring at the car wrecks and doesn't notice me.

"My father and Velma say hello," I say to let him know I'm here.

"Slow rolled, totaled, and the Robertson kid walks away without a scratch." He points to a blue Chevy Impala in the second row. He's thinking about Buddy, and I am too.

Before I got involved with Bruce I spent a lot of time hanging around Willard's Filling Station and Wrecker Service, hoping Buddy would notice me when he came down 25 driving the powerful tow truck with the red flashers blazing on the roof. He would lean on the horn to signal to his father that he was coming and then he would pull around behind the station. Buddy could handle anything: Sevilles, Thunderbirds, Continentals, little foreign cars. In one maneuver he would align the wreck next to another, then, releasing the winch slowly, set it down as carefully as if it were some new model on the showroom floor. If he saw me watching from the lean-to he would call, "Hi." I was so mesmerized by the way he swung out of the cab and landed springing like an astronaut on the moon, little puffs of dust rising around his boots, I could hardly wave back. Sometimes he didn't notice me because Route 25 where it joins the Interstate to Baltimore gets a lot of action and he would have to go out immediately on another call.

Uncle Willard picks up the beer bottle sweating on the bench. When he discovers it is empty he says, "How about us taking another look at the Impala?" There are several Impalas on the lot, but I know he has the two-door coupe in mind.

We walk together between the two rows of wrecks. The older ones huddled together in the sun look very peaceful with the goldenrod and wild phlox growing up around their wheels. The Impala, the last car Buddy towed, is at the end of the row on our right. Even from a distance the windshield, criss-crossed with threadlike cracks, and the headlights crushed into the grille, show what happened to the car.

"You had a tough job bringing this one in." Uncle Willard faces the car and touches the hood. The hot metal startles him and he pulls his hand away. "Really tough, wasn't it?"

"Sure was."

The first time Uncle Willard talked to me as if I were Buddy I felt weird, but then I realized he had seen me around the filling station day after day, so now when he drifts off I go along with him.

"Well, you did great." Uncle Willard starts to walk unsteadily back to the filling station. "Time for a beer."

Velma says he hasn't gone through the mourning process. Pretending I'm Buddy is a denial of reality. Velma is a moron. Love is like glue. It needs to stick to something.

I follow behind, hoping he won't stumble in the ruts. He is a tall man with long thin arms that swing out of sync with the rest of him. Although the sun has gone down, the air is still hot from the wrecks baking all day. Uncle Willard hunches over on the bench and cools his hands on the beer bottle while I sit on an old kitchen chair watching the ground fog settle at the far end of the lot where the land is low. The Impala looks like it's floating. The phone in the office behind us rings.

"Let it ring," Uncle Willard mumbles, and I do, but each ring triggers Bruce shouting "Wah wah wah" in my head. He is in a phone booth cruising under water with a map of Maryland on the dash. Even after the phone stops I have to get up and walk around to get rid of him.

"Something the matter?" Uncle Willard asks without looking up.

"No, I'm okay."

"You mustn't take on about your mother. The way I see it, when the plane dropped she just shoved you seat and all right out onto a snow bank." He takes a swallow of beer and then goes on calmly: "That blizzard saved you."

If I wasn't afraid of bursting into tears I'd reach over and grab his arm. A freak storm in the Appalachians caused the plane crash. Buddy and his mother—they were great ones for visiting relatives all over the country—did not survive, and the papers said that when the wreckage was located the dead were nothing but bones and ashes. There were no real bodies in spite of the coffins and heaps of flowers in Perrytown's funeral parlor, so when Uncle Willard talks so crazy it makes sense to me in spite of Velma and the newspapers.

"There's no way to figure accidents. Take that blue Impala for instance. Roof caved in, chassis a mess of spaghetti at the bottom of the embankment, and young Robertson taking a leak in the bushes. Not a scratch on him, at least not till the next day. Bushes full of poison ivy."

The bottle clinks against his teeth, and then I hear him say, "No poison ivy to bother you on that mountainside. Right?"

I don't answer. My breath is trapped somewhere under my ribs.

"How about another beer? Then we'll fix some supper."

In the shadows of the lean-to his voice is distant and gentle, but I'm frightened. I can't be Buddy any more. "Uncle Willard, it's me, Emily." I lean forward in my chair. He tilts his head away. He is drifting out of reach and taking me with him.

The air is suddenly cool and full of currents spiraling upwards. Geysers of snow foam around me, thrusting the chair higher and higher. Far below, Route 25 is a thin gray stripe on the hills, then disappears in white drifts. I feel weightless, wildly excited and happy like a child being tossed in a blanket. When I put out my hand to touch the streams of crystals brushing across my face, warm calloused fingers curl around my wrist.

"You're a good girl, Emily."

Uncle Willard's face blurs as I fall back and let the tears come. "I wish Buddy were here."

"Buddy's dead. I didn't want to say it but there's no point in your waiting for him."

"I know."

He lets go of my wrist. We sit silently in the dark. I feel limp, empty, as if I had been talking for hours, telling Uncle Willard all the things I meant to. How I can't get hold of my life, how everyone but me seems glued, my mother to Ralph and the kids on that sand bar, my father to Velma and her folks. Even Bruce, when I'm not around to fight with, has Maryland and his Barracuda. Uncle Willard doesn't know about Bruce and me. On account of Buddy I have skipped telling him that part of my life. Now it's getting late and Uncle Willard is too out of it to focus on me.

Something clicks overhead and the car lot is suddenly illuminated by floodlights.

"Time to lock up." Uncle Willard yawns and rubs

his eyes. "Meet you out front. I'll drive you home in the truck."

Swarms of tiny bugs bombard the lights over the gas pumps. Route 25 is empty. The gate to the chain link fence around the car lot clangs closed and then Uncle Willard calls that he is going to the apartment upstairs to look for the keys to the truck. He is absentminded about keys. Buddy always kept extra sets on a chain attached to his belt. I wait, listening to the bugs and the fluorescent lights ping and hum. I count the old tires piled next to a couple of oil drums near the road. Headlights coming from the direction of Perrytown pick out the drums. The car is coming fast. It stops suddenly across the road with a blast of *Maryland, My Maryland*.

"Hi," Bruce shouts from the open window. "Been looking for you."

"Sure, cruising," I'd like to shout back, but I can't. My tongue is paralyzed because I'm worrying about what to say if Uncle Willard appears and sees Bruce in the Barracuda with its gross chrome-plated wire wheels and moondust metallic paint. If Uncle Willard talks crazy, Bruce will ask, "Who the hell is Buddy?" because I've never told him about that part of my life, and then I'll have to.

"Get in," Bruce calls.

The cassette tape has run out, but the Barracuda roars as he revs the motor impatiently, and I feel that any minute we're going to fight. He opens the door opposite the driver's seat. "Let's go."

"I don't have time for cruising any more."

"Okay, I'll take you home. Look, I'm sorry about yesterday."

"You'll have to wait while I say good night to my uncle."

"Go ahead. No sweat." He shrugs and stiff-arms the steering wheel.

The stairs are dark, but the lights are on in the apartment, and I can hear Uncle Willard muttering to himself. He must be in the kitchen. I smell coffee brewing. Maybe he has forgotten about me, but I can't be sure.

"Good night, Uncle Willard. I'm going now."

"Good girl." He comes to the top of the stairs and starts down slowly. "Buddy'll drive you home."

I dash out. As Bruce puts the Barracuda in gear, I look back to the filling station. Uncle Willard is waving from inside the office. The red sign on the glass door says SORRY WE'RE CLOSED.

Day One

STAN HARPER had always stated his views on babies clearly. He dislikes them. Though given to occasional moods of dark silence, Stan was handsome, popular, and no one paid much attention to his anti-baby stance.

"It's just a pose," his mother would say to reassure the pretty girls in love with him.

He asked Jane Blake to be his bride, saying, "I love you, Jane Blake, but no babies ever."

"Why?" she wondered.

"They depress me. I hated being one."

"You can remember that far back?"

"I remember everything from day one."

As Stan foresaw, Jane dropped the subject. It had always amazed him that no one ever doubted his feat of memory, no one ever demanded details, something more concrete than his general disgust for the wetness, burps, and farts common to all newborns. Nobody, he concluded, wanted to be reminded of having been a baby.

He had been challenged only once to prove his claims. His mother had invited family and friends to a barbecue on the terrace to celebrate his twenty-fifth birthday. The guests were enjoying their drinks under the trees and he was poking at the charcoal when Sol Friedman, a smart-ass trial lawyer, yelled across the lawn, "Okay, birthday boy. I don't believe you remember a damn thing about your first days of life. Give us evidence, an event, a date."

Sol's raw boozy voice silenced all conversation. Stan spooned extra green chili sauce on the steaks and then, peering at Friedman through the smoke and sparks, said: "July 17, eight days after my birth, St. Joseph's Hospital. I was circumcised at 10 A.M. It hurt. Questions, anyone?"

Ice rattled noisily in glasses as men gulped their drinks. All the guests turned away from Sol as he zigzagged between them toward the barbecue.

"Fantastic, Stan, and you're not even Jewish," he roared, spilling most of his drink.

Stan flipped the steaks over and smiled. He wasn't telling that he hadn't the faintest recollection of being circumcised.

Shortly after the birthday party, Jane and Stan were married. They were happy; their widowed mothers, Andrea and Eileen, were happy.

Andrea and Eileen's friendship had begun at the edge of a sand box. They had been good mothers and now, still vigorous, they found that paddle tennis, garden club, and Jazzercise merely fed their hunger for a grandchild, a new life into which they could pour the love dammed to overflowing in their hearts. But there was no sign of a new life, and as the months passed, they began to fear that by the time a child appeared they would be so feeble, there would be nothing left of themselves to give.

Jane and Stan noticed what they called the frustrated granny look in the eyes of Andrea and Eileen. Jane told them: "Stan and I don't need a child to validate our relationship."

"Who's talking about validation?" Jane's mother said to Stan's mother on the phone later.

"Who's talking about relationships?" Stan's mother replied and then added, "Sounds like Woody Allen without the laughs."

On their third wedding anniversary Stan told Jane, "Our mothers make me feel guilty."

"Guilt is no reason to have a baby. Love is the only reason."

"And we really do love each other. Are you telling me that . . . ?"

"Yes. I'm pregnant, and yes, I know you don't like babies. Don't worry. I'll take care of everything."

The fact that Barnard Stillman Harper, the reddish-pulpy creature in the crib—Stan's old crib saved by his mother—was flesh of his flesh did nothing to lessen Stan's dislike. Little squint eyes looked up at him, hands waved erratically until a fist landed in the mouth, to be gummed greedily.

"Barney baby, look me up when you've stopped drooling and are ready to play catch," Stan said and kept out of the nursery.

He wasn't needed. Between Jane and the grandmothers, the baby was washed, oiled, changed, fed, burped, and passed from one pair of protective arms to another. The baby never cried. At the slightest whine one of the women would be at its side to jolly it until squeals and gurgles of contentment filled the home. This all-pervasive cheerfulness worried Stan.

"Your son is a happy baby. You were the same," his mother insisted.

He didn't contradict her. She had her memories to defend and to relive. She had presided over his infant years. Her lap, her lullabies had enclosed him, and whenever he claimed to remember all the miseries, she would simply smile and say, "You were an angel. You never cried."

"Sure, Mom, have it your way," he would say and kiss her.

He knew he had cried, wept secret tears quiet as whispers in the night while everyone slept, wept in rage at being toothless, speechless, and too weak to escape the bars of his crib. Heavy with tears, he had sunk into the darkness where voices joined his own in drawn-out cries like those of submerged creatures.

But now Barnard Stillman Harper was the focus of attention, and Stan found his days unencumbered by the chores of parenting. His golf and tennis partners, all young fathers, saw their games grow rusty as trips to the pediatrician, changes in feeding schedules, and other disruptions consumed their free time.

"Kronos ate his kids," Stan reminded them.

One Saturday afternoon in August, Stan was consoling himself over the collapse of his foursome with a stiff vodka and tonic as he stretched out on the living room chaise. Jane came in and announced, "Here's your chance to play father. Don't do a thing. If the baby wakes up before I get home, which he won't, turn him over and give him his juice. It's in the fridge next to the vodka."

Then she and the grandmothers were gone, taking with them those cooing, coaxing voices and the sounds of splashing water commingled with the squeaks of rubber toys and baby laughter. The house was suddenly silent. Stan's hand shook slightly as he raised his glass to finish his drink. Then he heaved himself to his feet and tiptoed to the doorway of the nursery. He had heard of crib death, how some infants quit breathing, just gave up without even a whimper. The baby lay on his stomach, his face turned away, revealing a bare spot of pink coming through the dark fuzz, where his head had been rubbed bald from lying on his back. Under the cotton undershirt the tiny torso pulsed. Stan breathed with it for a moment and then went into the kitchen.

The kitchen, with its old-fashioned white tiled walls and green awnings, was the coolest room in the house. The fridge hummed softly in its niche as he took out one of two bottles of vodka to make himself another drink. At first he thought the insistent rising and falling sound was the fridge working to reduce the heat he had let in, but then he realized it came from the baby's room. He rushed to the side of the crib and gently rolled the baby over on its back. Its belly pumped like a bellows, its compressed, wrinkled face was awash with tears from tightly closed eyes and drool from nose and mouth. Once on its back, the baby kicked its stunted legs, let out three screams, and then settled into a continuous wail.

Terrified, Stan searched to see if some sharp object had penetrated the baby's skin, but there was nothing of the kind in or even near the crib. Jane was very careful about sharp objects. He opened one side of the diaper: clean and dry, the only dry spot, in fact, because the kid was sweating as much as he was. Stan lifted the hot spongy baby up, placed it against his shoulder, and rubbed its back while he paced the floor.

"Come on, Barney, give us a burp and we'll both feel better."

The baby wriggled like a wet worm and yelled in his ear. Stan shifted to knee bouncing, patty cake, and a bit of tossing, but Barney would not be consoled.

"Okay, a bottle for you and a vodka for me, and if you don't settle down, I'll spike your juice," Stan said, and back at the kitchen table, with the baby cradled in one arm, he refilled his glass and then offered Barney the bottle of juice. After one swallow, the baby spat out the nipple and with brimming eyes resumed its wailing.

"Barney, I know it's hell." Stan shambled around the kitchen, rocking the baby and occasionally taking a swig of vodka straight from the bottle. His face oozed sweat and his eyes ached with unshed tears. "Barney, there are millions of you out there ready to bawl your hearts out, and there are millions of mothers and grandmothers begging you to smile like goddam angels. You and I know it's baby hell, a goddam vale of tears, and bawling is all a beginner can do, and here I am telling you not to, but listen to me and please don't bawl because I can't go through all that shit again."

The baby answered with sobs and rapid hiccups that shook its whole body.

Unable to trust his rubbery legs, Stan slumped onto the chair by the table and held the baby in his lap. Barney protested the sudden halt, stiffened his spine, and went into something between a wail and a moan which the tiled and metal surfaces of the kitchen amplified to a deafening level. Stan sat and filled his glass with the remaining vodka. Ice, he needed ice for a last drink. He leaned forward and with his free hand opened the door to the freezer compartment. Barney writhed and kicked him in the stomach. Through the blur of mist that clouded the frosted interior, Stan groped for a tray. Something stuck to his hand, burned in his palm so that he dropped it. The round container landed upright on the table. Haagen-Dazs. Chocolate. The only spoon he could find in the table drawer was a cluster of multicolored plastic measuring spoons. Propping Barney up in his lap, Stan dipped the red teaspoon into the ice cream and got a great glob of rich brown.

"Lick, don't bite," his mother had warned him. She didn't remember saying that. With four children tugging at her in front of the soda fountain, how could she be expected to remember the precise summer moment when he had held his first ice cream cone, grasped it with both hands as if it were a chalice filled to overflowing with a spire of cream. Raising it to his lips, he bit off the entire peak. As the cold seared the roof of his mouth, ached through his teeth to the bones of his jaws, he burst into tears from the shock and pain, then cried even louder with surprise and delight as the sweetness came through the pain and he tasted it for the first time melting on his tongue.

Now he licked the teaspoon clean. When he took a second spoonful, the measuring spoons jingled and the baby suddenly grabbed one of the cluster.

"Okay, why not, old buddy." Stan gently disengaged the tiny fingers and brought the heaped teaspoon to the baby's mouth.

"Lick, don't bite," Stan said, but Barney lurched forward.

When the ice cream slipped into his mouth, he gasped

for breath, twitched his nose, and swallowed. Then with a howl he tugged at the empty spoon.

Stan refilled it.

"LOOK AT THEM napping together on the chaise," Jane said from somewhere in the living room.

Stan kept his eyes closed and one hand on the baby, its face wedged up beside him.

"That poor child has been crying. Look at his cheeks, smeared with tears and chocolate ice cream," one grandmother lamented.

"They've both been crying," keened the other grandmother.

"They've been having a ball. Let them sleep it off," Jane said and left the room.

The house, filled with the hum of busy voices and running bath water, expanded and grew light as a bubble in the shadows of late afternoon.

Stan whispered: "Barney, this is day one. You'll forget all the baby crap, the sniffling and dumb giggling in your crib. Now you know what's really out there and now you're part of it along with me. When it hurts, and there's lots of hurt, bawl your head off. And when it's sweet, go for it. This is the beginning, the day you'll remember."

Without opening his eyes, Barney put a sticky fist in his mouth and Stan dozed while the chaise floated undisturbed above the grandmothers, who were calling, "Bath time, supper's ready."

The Wet Sidewalk

HAZY WITH SLEEP, she senses the bed is not hers. The hollow in the mattress is too deep; the pillow is rubbery and hot, and the bed is listing. She wakes up shocked that under the tangled sheet she is naked.

The room is full of shadows except near a window where a small round table and two wooden chairs huddle in pale light. She remembers sitting or trying to sit on one of the chairs. Armless, straight-backed, it had offered no support, and she had felt too shaky to risk any movement beyond leaning her elbows on the table. A half-empty whiskey bottle and two glasses, one over-turned, are still on the table. She raises her head to look for her clothes and a spasm of nausea blurs her vision. The bottle and glasses shimmy noiselessly. Sickened, she closes her eyes. The darkness, abrupt and soothing now, had been terrifying when the elevator jerked to a halt and the sound of metal scraping metal filled the airless cabin.

"Don't panic. I'll get it going." A small light in the ceiling came on, illuminating a young bearded face. She felt her gut tighten. Robert had always cautioned her about parking lots, garages, and elevators if she came home alone at night. He used to worry whenever business took him out of town, leaving her on her own.

"Press the red button." She pointed to the panel just above his shoulder. "That'll wake the super."

"Cool it, lady. I know how this thing works." He held a small wrench in his hand. "I seen you around. You were at Louie's tonight."

She didn't like the idea of his watching her drinking alone at the bar, a quiet neighborhood place near the apartment. Before the accident, she and Robert had often gone there for a nightcap. It comforted her to go back. Friends disapproved, cautioned her against giving in to loneliness and dwelling on the past. "We understand, Laura. Such a terrible loss, but you're still young." They didn't understand. Grief was her link to Robert. Like the phantom pain of a severed limb, grief kept him present. When people, intending to be kind, said "Time is a great healer," she turned away, taking her grief with her, sheltering it so that each day it grew deeper, like love.

With the arrival of summer, friends phoned from the country. "Come anytime," they insisted. Her older sister, Liz, called early every morning, waking her up, urging her to pull herself together. "You've got to get out, Laura. See people." But Laura drew the shades against the gritty heat on the penthouse terrace. She came out in the evenings, and then only to go to Louie's. A few drinks muted the sirens, distanced the cop's face popping in and out of the darkness with the flashing lights of squad cars and ambulances.

Overhead, the light flickered and a fan began to stir the dead air in the elevator.

"Sure, I seen you in the lobby." He put the wrench in his pocket and pressed one of the buttons.

The elevator dropped, throwing her off balance. Seeing him step toward her, she staggered back against the metal wall in terror.

"Take it easy. We can have a drink in my place and then I'll ride you up to your apartment, OK?" He reached out and gently linked her arm in his. The gesture was so unexpectedly kind, the voice so soft, she began to cry. The elevator door sucked open, and clinging to him she stepped out into the basement corridor and let him lead her to his room. His arm was hairless, muscular. He slipped it around her waist, easing her down, his movements slow and quiet, part of the shadows.

On the windowsill the light has grown pearly. Turning on her side, she sees a night table and next to it a twin bed. The sheet drawn up to the headboard covers a body. White folds join in deep gashes of shadow between the legs. No blood on the stretcher. No movement.

Fully awake now, she reaches down between the beds for her clothes. Panty hose, bra. Standing makes her dizzy, and she grabs the back of one of the wooden chairs. A smell of whiskey rises from the table top.

"Get outta here."

The tone from the bed behind her is edgy, impatient.

"I can't find my purse, my keys."

"Here."

The purse lands on the table. The wallet is missing.

Laura looks back at the bed. A head and naked torso appear from under the sheet. A bluish red blotch, a birth mark or a tattoo, she can't make out which, colors one upper arm.

"My door key. In the coin purse of my wallet."

He sits up and takes the green leather wallet from the night table drawer. "You sure keep a lot on you." He lets her watch him slowly remove the bills.

Since Robert's death she has taken to carrying too much cash. "Always put the large denominations in a separate place in your purse," he told her. The money disappears into the night table drawer. It's her fault. Robert had warned her to be careful. It's all her fault. Last night, the drinks at Louie's, the man in the elevator.

"Catch," he says.

The wallet falls at her feet. She retrieves it and looks for her shoes. One is on the floor by the window, the other half hidden under an unpainted bureau. As she picks it up, she notices a photograph of a woman on the bureau. The features: small mouth, short blonde hair with a spiky cowlick, seem vaguely familiar, but she is too frantic to look closely.

Across the room he is getting dressed. White shirt, trousers, shoes. She struggles to locate him in the unclear memory of last night, but the white uniform throws her off. The man last night was wearing something dark. "You're an intern?"

The question triggers an angry glance. "Yeah, medical school on my dad's unemployment and food stamps. Even with a scholarship you gotta live." He zips up his fly. "I was going to be like those guys in *MASH*. Save lives, do surgery. All that healing hands crap. After six months my money ran out and I dropped out." He points to the red badge on his shirt pocket. "I'm a paramedic. I keep 'em alive on the way to the hospital."

The white figure, thin face with dark eyes emerge from a street crowd pressing around the ambulance. "Your name and address?" a deep voice asks.

"Laura Holden, 50 East 72nd. Let me through. That's my husband. I must go with him."

A woman in a uniform is holding her back while the stretcher is being covered.

"Okay, lady, keep calm," the man says.

Now she recognizes him. "You were there when Robert . . ." She slumps against the bureau and closes her eyes against the sight of him that night and last night.

"Come on, take your things and get outta here." His voice—she hears it shouting orders, clearing the way for the stretcher—is impatient.

"I'm going." She moves away from him, and gripping the shoe as if it were a weapon, limps to a chair. "As soon as I catch my breath. There's no air in here."

"It's sure no penthouse like you're used to."

He moves around the room restlessly, pressing her to hurry. "I gotta go to work, and while you're sitting up there on that terrace all by your widow lonesome don't get any ideas. I felt sorry for you last night. I remembered you at Louie's with him, you smiling into his face like you was Nancy Reagan smiling at Ron."

"You watched us?"

"Plenty of times. Seen you outside the building waiting while he flagged a cab and then helped you in. A real gent."

She drops the shoe and presses the back of her hand against her mouth, forcing the knuckles between her teeth to stifle the thought of him spying on her and Robert with his starved eyes.

"Last night, I wasn't going to touch you, just have a whiskey and take you upstairs. Hell, you wouldn't of missed the money. But you started crying when I gave you my arm and I felt sorry for you. Dumb bastard wanted to help."

A loud buzzing fills the room. Frightened, she looks up.

"Come on, move it." He shuts off the alarm clock on the night table. "Nan'll be here any minute. We can't be late on the job." He tosses a woman's uniform on one of the beds and starts pulling the sheets off the other.

She stands up and slips her foot in the shoe. "You and she work together?"

"We're a team, day and night." He laughs, barely opening his lips. "This yours?" He steps on the blue suede belt to her dress.

She nods, and he kicks it across the floor. "Okay now, beat it."

She picks up the belt, puts her wallet in her purse and faces him. "What if I report you to the police?"

"Sure, and how you got loaded and spent the night here in the sack." He crams the sheets into a pillowcase. "Naw, you'll keep your mouth shut like all the others."

"The others?"

"Lots." He throws the pillowcase in a corner and focuses his anger on her. "This is death city, lady. Every sixty-seven seconds a fatality. Homicides, suicides, accidents, I seen 'em all and the survivors too. Nan consoles the men, I take care of the women. Women like you, with money." He grabs the pillow and slaps it into shape. "One of these days I'm splitting for those beaches in California." He presses the pillow to his chest, half-smiling rides the white surf, catches the big one just right. The crest crumbles. The smile crumbles. The dark head jerks up. "Go back to that penthouse where you belong. You got more than your money's worth last night. Now out before I throw you out." He yanks the door to the corridor open.

The penthouse is cool and silent. She goes out onto the terrace. To the east beyond the river a hazy radiance colors the horizon of smokestacks and warehouses. On the avenue below, a garbage truck mawing black plastic sacks edges its way uptown. The side streets are empty, the store fronts dark behind steel grilles. She leans over the wall. Beneath the terrace, the side of the building drops unobstructed, its gray stone as smooth as a slide. She leans farther out and feels the pull, sees herself suddenly weightless, the air cool and buoyant as water, and her falling body dissolving in the stream of ashen particles that drift down onto the city pavements.

The phone in the kitchen is ringing. Liz's wake-up call. She closes her mind to it and concentrates on the street below where the super is hosing down the section of sidewalk in front of the building. A small white dog pulls against a leash held by a little girl; it refuses to cross the wet strip. The child stops, looks back, waits. The super, his bald head bobbing over the concrete, waves them on. The dog only wags its tail and sits down.

All three of them are in her way. If she stands on the wall now, the girl might look up and see her. The super would shout and call the police. She wants quiet, the protective quiet Robert always provided. The super steps aside and lets the hose run freely from the doorstep to the gutter. As she watches the water spread a clear film over the swept stone, she is suddenly conscious of her throat tight with thirst, of her breasts and thighs sticky under her clothing. She leaves the terrace and goes into the kitchen. The tap water is lukewarm. She waits until it turns cold, then leans over the sink and washes her face, rinses her mouth before drinking from cupped hands. But the odor of tobacco still clings to her fingers, the sour taste of alcohol coats her tongue. The phone stops ringing. Perhaps her sister will think she has at last gone to visit friends and has spent the night with them in the country. She returns to the terrace and looks down: the sidewalk is deserted now, the wet surface glassy in the morning light. She climbs onto the wall, crouches like a swimmer, and pushes off into the clean emptiness below.

Flying Home

FLYING WAS what my father knew and loved. "Never marry," he would advise me long before I was old enough to understand the meaning of the married state. He mystified me further with talk of wind-sheer passions, uncontrolled spins and dives, factors that apparently had something to do with my being on earth and his child. At the end of these monologues he would give me a hug and tell me about how it was with him and her before I was born. He told a good story, my father did, and relived those early days with each telling.

After he got out of the air force, he continued to fly, although as a former fighter pilot he found spraying crops dull. However, the work paid well and left him time for skywriting.

My mother, a new bride, complained that he never let her fly with him.

"I love you too much. Skywriting is dangerous and I'm still learning the alphabet," he explained.

"Then you're crazy to take chances when everything just melts in the air."

She was right, of course. On a good day his best efforts dissolved in less than thirty minutes and all he had to show were wisps of haze.

"I'm working on a new system. It's a secret, but when I've perfected it, you'll be amazed," he told her.

The day he completed a Z, she was waiting on the ground.

"So now what are you going to write?" she asked.

"I'll think of something," he said and took off again.

After she walked out on him, he plastered her name all over the sky. Elaine was not an easy name. The E's tended to fade quickly and the L to topple over. Air pockets and thermals distorted the letters. One time he looked back up and read PAIN. On windy days he simply wrote ♡, which could be accomplished in a single maneuver.

One afternoon the weather was ideal, his technique flawless. He soared until ED LOVES ELAINE filled the sky. When he returned home, the inscription was still in place though starting to blur. While he stood admiring his achievement from the back porch, the phone rang.

"Quit it," Elaine snarled.

"Not quitting," he snarled back. Since taking up sky writing, he spoke in short phrases.

"You're a nut," she said and hung up.

The complaint pleased him. It meant he was getting to her and to that guy she was living with, Eric the roofer, who never left the ground without something solid under him. Eric must have seen the skywriting above every roof in the area.

The morning after Elaine's call, a low ceiling and falling barometer made flying inadvisable. He spent the day at the kitchen table studying plans to refit his plane so he could write in bold rainbow colors that would remain in the atmosphere for hours.

By evening, clouds like enormous bruises discolored the sky. The house seemed lonelier than ever in the storm. Rain pelted the windows and the wind probed every seam of the frame siding. He went from room to room checking for leaks. The roof worried him. He had flown over villages hit by a hurricane. The roofless homes had stood like dollhouses, their interiors intact but every secret exposed. If his roof went, he would live in the cellar rather than let Eric nail down a single shingle. As he returned to the kitchen to heat a can of soup for supper, the lights flickered. He had just enough time to open the drawer in the kitchen table before the power went out. The drawer was empty. Elaine had taken the candles with her. With a flashlight and a bottle of Bourbon he sat in darkness. Eric's house would be cheerful with a fire burning in the wood stove and Elaine smiling in candlelight under a tight roof. He fell into bed fully dressed, in case he had to make for the cellar.

In the morning he awoke chilled. The air was so frigid, he opened his eyes expecting to see sky, but the roof was in place. Wrapping a blanket around his shoulders, he hurried into the kitchen and turned on the stove. It was working. He had just taken the eggs out of the icebox when the phone rang. Elaine was on the line screaming, "You've got to quit it." Then the roofer came on, cursing through a mouthful of nails.

"You're both nuts. I haven't done a thing. I just got out of bed," he yelled.

"Liar. Take a look outside," Elaine sobbed.

He hung up and went out onto the back porch. In the aftermath of the storm, the sunlight was brilliant. A current of cold air drew white clouds across the glacial blue of the sky. At the zenith they glistened in letters as bright and sharp as icicles: ELAINE LOVES ED.

His invention of skywriting in rainbow colors remained a dream, because he didn't need it. After she saw that glittering declaration, she couldn't resist him and came home to make a baby.

He continued to fly but stopped writing love to her after I was born and Eric fell fatally off a barn roof.

At my first cries, "Where's Daddy?" my mother would point to birds, robins in spring, crows year round. I got the idea. Daddy flies.

Stunt pilot, carnival ace, he soared above our lives, a winged god who rarely touched the ground. She waited, read clouds for a clue to his whereabouts, and listened for the step on the stair that my calico, Delilah, always heard first. Delilah met him at the door in her own good time. No fuss, no welcoming show. She sensed what we pretended not to know. On every flight he found a bird.

NOW, ON A VISIT I hear my adult and married self asking still, "Dad home?"

"Always, these days." Mother puts her needlework aside and waves him in from the garden.

"They can find their own damned nectar," he declares, testing her and the familial atmosphere for turbulence.

Her tapestry needle threads green in and out of Eden, an earthly paradise where the lion—Delilah's twin in satin—lies with the lamb, the eagle nests with the dove.

Mother won't be disturbed by his comings and goings any more than are the hummingbirds who shun the sugar-water vials he has hung on a palm (her idea to busy him in his retirement). The birds prefer flowers.

"Noon, *my* nectar time." He hums, flaps his elbows, and downs the whiskey neat.

By dinnertime he flies, logs mileage hours in his head. A night flight over Eden. On the horizon a moon casts sequin light on fronds of green moiré.

At dinner time she says, "All done," and holds up the finished appliqué. Boozy, he glides by, motors dead, an old stunt, to graze the trees.

"Something's wrong," he shouts. "You've left out something."

"Just the sky." She snips a last thread.

I wait in the garden for the turbulence to pass. Delilah prowls a flower bed of all the sweetness Eden promises. Her prey darts. The wings, invisible in flight, hum.

I reenter the house. He's home. Dinner is late.

Vital Signs

THE SOUND, a burred, insistent pulse, bore in upon her. Struggling out of sleep, she forced her senses to accept the abrasive rhythm while she searched the crumpled shadows for a point of reference: night table, clock, its dimly lit face half hidden by a cluster of medicine bottles. The sound, confined within gray walls, grew louder. Alert now, she recognized it. Snoring. He was snoring vigorously. Lungs and heart pumping hard: a body's vital signs.

Relieved, she lay still, wondering if perhaps he was playing possum, breathing like that in order to wake her without seeming to. She raised her head to scrutinize the face in the next bed. The eyes were closed, the brows drawn together at the bridge of the nose: the tension of pain working against the medication. At the force of his exhalations the nostrils trembled. Illness had drained the fullness from his cheeks, giving the thin nose and bearded chin an exaggerated prominence. She had hoped he would never notice the alteration, but of course he knew his face too well. All his life he had studied, molded it to suit Punch, Bottom, Pickwick. This transformation was not of his making, and he fought it.

One morning while trying to shave himself in bed with her help, he had grabbed the can of shaving cream and sprayed a white band the length of his face, adding with a final flourish a peak of foam in the center of his forehead. "And that, best beloved, is how the unicorn came to be." He had an entire repertoire of impersonations learned in his early days, from the circus, Disneyland, TV commercials. Clowns and comical rabbits had led the way to Arden Forest, leading roles—Cyrano, Falstaff—and critical praise and awards. Since his illness he had taken to springing the comedy routines of his youth on her. She encouraged these antics, his own vital signs, and that morning the unicorn had been especially deserving of applause. Instead, she handed him a wet washcloth and left the room. The sight of the ravaged features breaking through a mask of runny shaving cream was more than she could bear. Nothing had prepared her to become his only audience.

Recently the clowning stopped, but he was in constant need of her presence, especially in the early morning hours when he would drift out of a drugged sleep. Then she would have to find a way to combat his anxiety, his depression. "Leave me." "Don't leave me." The fears that in lucid moments he hid from her. Now in the harsh throb of his snores she heard echoes of her own unspoken, "Don't suffer. Sleep. Die. Don't die." He turned toward her in the bed and, once on his side, breathed more peacefully. Reassured, she lay back on her pillow.

Through the open window at the foot of her bed she gazed at the apartment building across the street. A fanciful Gothic structure, the recesses of its facade were inhabited by basilisks and griffons just now emerging in the faint morning light. On good days he found the menagerie entertaining. As she drowsed, she heard a sound, an airy swish intermingled with the rise and fall of his breathing. She opened her eyes. Nothing stirred in the shadows of the bedroom. She got out of bed and went to the window. Daylight had not yet reached the street, empty except for parked cars hugging the curb beneath the amber glow of the street lights. Seen from above, the dark glossy bodies resembled seals basking in the sun. All silent.

On the sidewalk parallel to a black limousine she noticed a gray oblong shape, possibly a VW parked illegally in the protective shadow of a hearse. It shifted slowly toward the middle of the sidewalk, and again she heard the curious swish as the elephant raised its head and trunk. A small elephant with a hide like pearl-gray felt, it strolled along fanning the air with its ears and furling and unfurling its trunk. A ginkgo directly beneath her window attracted its attention. She leaned over the sill, curious to see what it would make of the grimy city tree.

"Where are you?"

She turned into the room. He was lying on his back, his head tilted forward.

"I'm here. Don't worry."

"What are you doing?"

"There's a baby elephant under the ginkgo. I've been

watching it. Maybe when you're better, you can get up and . . ."

He smiled. "Maybe if you see a unicorn."

His head, pale and skeletal, fell back: Open-mouthed, he began to snore.

When she looked out the window again, the elephant had crossed the street. She lost sight of it behind a station wagon.

Weather Reports

"WHAT'S IT DOING?" Robert asks apprehensively, coming out on the patio where I am watching a dark, bloated cloud that squats like a gigantic toad on the Sangre de Cristo mountains.

"Nothing. It's doing nothing."

Relieved, he stretches out on a chaise. He has just arrived from the bland climate of Los Angeles and is unfamiliar with the caprices of summer weather in northern New Mexico. Since he has enough worries, I don't tell him that a cloud doing nothing, just sitting there on the Sangres, isn't normal. Here the sky is more restless than the sea, the landscape in continuous flux. Summer storms explode and engulf mesas with red dust, transforming them into dark islands. At sunset the clouds writhe like paper catching fire. A couple of years ago, after my husband died, I moved here, an urban Easterner attracted by the beauty of the desert but unaware of the turbulent summers. The Sangre de Cristos are my comfort.

"Blood of Christ," he says from the chaise. "Sounds awfully grim."

"Not really. To the Spanish it suggests salvation. You'll see this afternoon."

Rolling and wooded, the mountains form the eastern horizon. A fresh green in the morning, at the end of the day they reflect the fiery violence of the western sky, tempering it to a delicate rose. Now with the sun at its zenith, the green crests should pale, but the cloud darkens them. A dusty breeze crosses the patio; the brick floor and low adobe wall are still cool, deceptively cool.

"You'd better move into the shade," I caution him. "With your fair skin you're a prime candidate for skin cancer. The sun is lethal at this altitude."

He gives me a haunted look as I go into the house to catch the noon radio forecast. "Hot, clear, occasional afternoon showers possible." A carefully hedged prediction. By afternoon anything is possible. I listen out of habit.

In my family we are all weather-conscious, not in any scientific sense but by way of locating each other in some recognizable context. I have sisters and cousins scattered all along the East Coast. We phone on holidays and birthdays, and after the greetings and news one of us asks, "What is your weather doing?" When it's my turn to answer, my loved one can't place me. "Snowing? I thought you lived in the Sun Belt." They confuse Santa Fe with Phoenix. "Hail in June. Crazy." Unintentionally they leave me feeling cut off, the lone southwesterner in the desert.

From the kitchen I can see him lying on the chaise. The sun has crept up his legs. I regret having mentioned skin cancer. He is limp with fatigue. His wife Ann has left him after eight years of marriage. She is three months pregnant at the age of thirty-nine.

"No note. She just vanished," he told me when he called from California weeks ago.

The news stunned me. My instant reaction was silent rage at Ann. Robert is like a member of my family. We grew up together in Baltimore: same day school, summer camp. My mother is his godmother. He and I have always been close and over the years have kept in touch, meeting rarely after he moved to Los Angeles but speaking frequently on the phone. Robert calls me from his office to get news and gossip about relatives and old friends back in Baltimore. Ann never calls. I read about her and her innumerable social activities in the alumnae bulletin. She is a native Californian but came East to college. That's where we met.

"The cleaning woman saw her leave in a taxi," Robert reported.

Cars are easier to trace than people, and the fact that Ann had left hers behind suggested to me she wanted to make it difficult for him to find her. He was frantic, spending his days consulting the police and private investigators and then waiting for the phone to ring.

"It's only me," I said quickly whenever I called. "Any news?"

"None."

Weeks passed. The Sangres shed the last spring snow, and I worried with him and about him. I have always known Ann to have a harum-scarum streak and the fact that Robert met her through me made me feel somehow

47

responsible. I had introduced them at a cocktail party given jointly by Robert's parents and mine to welcome my fiancé into the fold. Ann had flown in from Los Angeles, arriving a bit late because of a snowstorm in the Baltimore area and making a significant impression on all the guests with her glowing suntan and outgoing manner.

At the end of the evening my mother had commented, "I didn't realize that you and that blonde girl from California were so close."

"We aren't. Ann collects people. In college she majored in being popular. I am just one of a legion of her dearest best friends."

"I hope she doesn't add my godson to her collection and lure him to California. Young lawyers, especially someone as conscientious as Robert, work long hours. That girl strikes me as wanting constant attention."

"That's what all those best friends are for."

When Robert and Ann married a year later, Mother and I decided it was a good match. Ann's demands and unpredictable behavior kept him interested; his even temper steadied her. In the early years of their marriage their Christmas cards showed them bronzed and smiling on a beach or in a sailboat. Eventually these scenes were replaced by a photograph of them against the background of a construction site. My mother noted that Robert had lost his suntan and looked thin in his California casuals. The following Christmas, Ann and Robert disappeared from the photograph. Instead, a handsome mission-style house stood on an extensive lawn. At first my mother said that at least Robert didn't live on a beach or in a boat, that he had made a proper home for himself. She did find the landscaping wanting. Apart from two or-

namental orange trees, not a pansy or a petunia interrupted the monotony of the lawn. When in subsequent
years the identical picture with printed greetings arrived,
my mother would scrutinize it and ask me, "Where is
Robert?" After I reminded her that he had phoned as
he always did at Christmastime, she would throw the
card away and accept my reassurances that all was well
in the white house with the tiled roof.

I had no reason to think otherwise until five weeks
ago, when Robert reported Ann's disappearance. As the
strain and fatigue showed increasingly in his voice, I
urged him to come for a weekend.

"It's only a two-hour flight. You can leave my number
with the police."

He hesitated but finally agreed.

"I'll be there tomorrow. What's the weather like?"

"Wonderfully unpredictable. Bring a sweater and dark
glasses."

The sun has now reached his bare forearms folded
across his chest. My neighbor, Mrs. Ortiz, is standing in
the shade of her portal watching the cloud. Water rates
have gone up again, and she's trying to decide whether
or not to water her garden, a random plantation of
hollyhocks, tomatoes, cosmos, and squash. She goes back
indoors. I can't leave him lying there unprotected while
I go into town to get something for dinner.

"Thanks." He opens his eyes at the sound of my
moving the umbrella. "Sorry to be such a drag."

"It's the altitude. Go back to sleep."

On my return from shopping I find him pacing back
and forth on the patio. His face is gray.

"Ann called," he says the minute he sees me. "She's
filed for a divorce. I don't understand what's happening."

He halts in the center of the patio and stares at me with the look of a drowned man, open-eyed, seeing nothing.

Across the road Mrs. Ortiz is shutting her windows.

"Let's go indoors." I close the umbrella.

We sit side by side on the living room sofa, facing the view of the mountains through the patio door. Sporadic lightning veins the cloud.

"Where did Ann call from?"

"Los Angeles, but she's going back to Mexico today. Wouldn't tell me where, except that she's found some clinic specializing in late pregnancies. She's been having problems. High blood pressure, kidneys."

I try to suggest something positive but do it without conviction. Ann would be a pushover for any quack.

"I called her doctor after she hung up on me. He says the treatment—diet and vitamins—isn't harmful but it's inadequate and he doubts she'll go to term."

"She can't be serious about a divorce. Not now. Perhaps it's her way, under stress, of making sure of you, of asking . . ."

"No." He gets up and goes to stand in the patio doorway. "I tried to reason with her, to explain . . ."

"Explain what?"

"She thinks you and I . . ."

"That's ridiculous," I burst out, glaring at the back of his head. "She could have reached you at home ages ago instead of letting you agonize over where she was." Unable to see his face, I am shouting, pleading shamelessly. "You and I are friends. She's using me as an excuse."

"Using my being here." He turns and faces me as I walk over to him. "I shouldn't have come, Harriet. I'm sorry."

"For God's sake don't be sorry." I'm exasperated at

his ready acceptance of blame from all sides when he should defend himself, and me, and our friendship.

"Okay," he smiles and, ignoring my anger, puts an arm around my shoulders.

The tip of his nose is bright red. It looks frostbitten.

"I'm glad I came. How about you?"

I manage a quick, "Of course," and step away. "Now help me water the geraniums on the patio."

The cloud has turned a soft mother-of-pearl and lies banked into the curves of the mountains. They are luminous, a shade of pale ruby.

I hand him the hose. "Once I turn on the water, you can adjust the nozzle. But first, look at the Sangres."

He takes the hose but isn't listening, isn't looking. "You know, Ann might just pull this one off, in spite of what her doctor thinks. If it's a girl, we'll name her Harriet." He smiles into some sunny future.

I give the faucet an angry twist. Under the sudden pressure the hose snakes violently in his hand, drenching him.

"Christ," he swears and drops it.

After he changes his clothes, we start for the airport in silence. Dark shadows spill out of the arroyos on either side of the road and spread across the desert lowlands. Robert shudders and rolls up the window.

"Didn't you bring a sweater? It gets cold the instant the sun goes down."

"I'm okay." He stares at the road. "I realize I've let you down, Harriet, but it's hard to make Ann understand. She doesn't have any friends."

"Now I don't understand. Ann has always been popular."

"She still is. The house is constantly full of people. I can't keep track of the new faces at our dinner table."

I get the picture—Ann, the tireless hostess of the Pacific Coast—but the picture darkens when he adds, "Ann burns people out. The turnover is terrific."

"A baby will make a great difference to both of you," I say to end his visit on an optimistic note.

He picks up on my cheerfulness and begins to plan a strategy for tracing Ann. There can't be many prenatal clinics that cater to foreigners in Mexico. Her doctor in Los Angeles will be able to locate the one she is going to. And anyway now, with this talk of divorce, her lawyer must have an address. If necessary he will fly the lawyer and the doctor to Mexico with him and bring her home.

I agree: that ought to make an impression.

"Is the airport much further?" He looks at his watch.

"Relax. We'll be there with time to spare." The road is good but in this half-light the visibility isn't the greatest. "If you're cold, there's a raincoat I always keep on the back seat."

He wraps the raincoat around his shoulders and looks out the window. "What's the name of those mountains over there you told me are so beautiful?"

"Sangre de Cristo."

"They're almost black now. Do they really turn the color of blood?"

"They did an hour ago. Too bad you missed it."

"I remember the cloud. It's still there."

He leans back in his seat and half closes his eyes. "Maybe it will bring rain. The mountains probably don't get much rain in this climate. Yet everything looks much greener than I expected, much greener than the hills around L.A.," he muses, drifting into the seared California landscape.

I step on the accelerator. The sudden speed jolts him back to the present, and as the lights of the airport come in view he sheds the raincoat and gropes in his pockets for his ticket. At the terminal we part hurriedly, a quick hug in the car and promises to keep in touch.

The storm breaks just as I step onto my portal. From a purple-black sky the rain falls so hard, it bounces off the glass of the patio door. My geraniums droop. Mrs. Ortiz's round face appears at a lighted window and then disappears as the wind drives a torrent between our houses. The storm moving from west to east merges the mountains, sky, and horizon into a formless dark. The phone rings. Ann's, "Harriet, I've been calling and calling," catches me so by surprise, all I can think to say is, "Robert isn't here."

"I need to talk to you, Harriet," she sobs. "It's been such ages."

"Ann, are you all right?"

"Fine, I'm doing fine. The medication makes me drowsy."

"Where are you?"

"Home." Ann's "home" is cheerless. The house is empty. "Friends were going to drive me to Cuernavaca but they dropped out at the last minute. I don't care. Mexico is no fun if one can't speak Spanish. Guess I'll have the baby here in English. I want a girl but the doctor says it will be a boy. Girls are much more company, don't you think?"

"Ann, the important thing is that you stay home and take care of yourself."

When she doesn't answer, I am frantic for fear she has left the phone off the hook and gone in search of better company.

"Ann, listen. I took Robert to the airport hours ago. He's on his way home."

"It's raining really hard where you are, Harriet," Ann says.

"Yes, a summer storm. How did you know?"

"I've got this radio station on that reports the weather twenty-four hours a day from all over the country."

I want to reach Ann, to offer her more comfort than a radio voice tracking the jet stream, but she is talking compulsively and I don't dare interrupt for fear of losing her.

"I tune in to all the places where I have friends. Right now it's raining in Santa Fe, Atlanta, El Paso. You remember Mimi Harper."

I don't recall any Mimi Harper, Bobby Woods, or the Hall twins who have red hair, but apparently we are all linked together by rain.

"Los Angeles is smoggy. No change predicted," she sighs.

"It's clearing here. Come for a visit after the baby is born. Mountain air and lots of interesting people."

The radio voice behind her grows louder. Barometric pressure in Bangor is steady. My sister lives in Bangor. Ann is silent. Maybe she doesn't have any best friends in Maine.

While waiting for her to pick up the phone again, I watch the night sky open and release a scattering of stars. White haze drifts between the moon and the crest of the Sangres. I hear a click. The radio voice fades.

"Bye," Ann says. "Robert's at the door."

Mrs. Ortiz has come out onto her lighted portal. I wave from the patio door and then hurry to move my flowerpots away from the rainwater still dripping from the canales on the roof. The phone rings. That will be Robert calling to say he has found Ann. I let it ring and hope their next Christmas card will be a sunlit picture of baby Robert.

The Good Women

"A SAINT, the woman's a saint," my mother says, and Gran, if she's awake, nods. I keep my mouth shut. The saint is Reverend Mother who lives in the convent attached to the Home for the Aged. She used to run the home but now she's retired and just prays all the time. Whenever anything really bad happens to our family, like when the baby died in his crib or father was killed working in the subway, Mother reminds me, "Reverend Mother is praying for us. God hears her." Reverend Mother and Gran grew up together and have been friends for a zillion years. After father died and we had to move to this apartment over Walkowicz's Deli, my sister Kathy complained a lot. We don't have any friends in the neighborhood or at school and the apartment is crummy, but I don't care because the convent is only six blocks away which means that Gran, although she has a bad heart and a bad ankle, can visit her old friend.

From the empty lot behind the gas station on the corner you can see the steeple of the chapel and the tall pointed windows of the convent parlor where we wait when we take Gran to see Reverend Mother. The parlor looks like a skating rink; the nuns must wax the floor every day. The only furniture is a long table with claw feet and straight chairs that have carvings on the backs. I always sit on the edge of my chair. The red plush covering on the seat is so worn, I'm afraid it might pull out of the brass nails, and then Reverend Mother would see right through me to the torn place.

While we wait, Kathy squirms, Gran dozes next to the armchair at the head of the table, and opposite her, Mother says the rosary silently on her fingers. The nuns' habits rustle outside the parlor door. Sometimes we hear moaning. Mother says many of the aged are senile and they act kind of crazy. Once when I had to go down the hall to the bathroom I met an old woman who was almost bald. She pointed at me and then pulled her skirt up over her head. I locked the bathroom door and stayed there until one of the nuns coaxed her back upstairs to her room. Since then I always go to the bathroom even if I don't need to before we leave for the convent.

When Reverend Mother opens the parlor door and hurries across the polished floor, we all stand up. I poke Kathy to remind her to curtsy. Reverend Mother is very tall, and from the way the wooden rosary with the silver crucifix hangs around her waist I can tell that she's thin as a stick. Unlike the young nuns, she wears the old-style habit of her order, a long white tunic over a white robe with wide sleeves, a veil and a wimple that hides her face in profile. All these white layers and hems fill the space around her. She sits in the armchair at the head of the table and talks to Gran and Mother. Then Sister Ann, who has a fat red face and thick legs, brings Kathy and me a plate of dry yellow cookies that smell of vanilla. The convent is very poor and the nuns save all the butter and eggs for the aged. After we eat the cookies we sit with our hands in our laps until Reverend Mother stands up and promises to remember us in her prayers. Saying goodbye makes Gran weepy, but Reverend Mother's eyes are like two steel balls. I keep my eyes on the bottom hem of her habit.

We haven't been to visit Reverend Mother since Christmas. For the past two months Gran hasn't been well. She seems to have shrunk and all she can do is sit by the window and look at the fire escape. The weather in Purgatory must be like January and February here: dirty boring slush. Her ankle aches and the heart medicine makes her sleepy. Some afternoons after school I put an ice pack on the ankle which is very swollen and a horrible purple where the bone juts out. I wrap the ice pack in a clean dish towel, and although I try my best not to hurt her she flinches and holds her breath when the lumpy cold touches the skin. After I take care of Gran I go pick a fight with Kathy or lock myself in the bathroom and gorge on my secret store of peanut brittle to help me forget Gran's suffering. I love her so much, I can feel her pain eating through my head down into my ankle until I want to scream and smash the bathroom mirror, let the tub overflow and flood the stairs down into Walkowicz's Deli and on to the whole street.

Gran does have good days even in January and February. Her mind is clear and she wants to go out, but every time mother calls the convent she is told Reverend Mother can't see us.

"How come?" I ask when she comes upstairs from the pay phone in the deli.

"It's not a good time," is all she will answer.

Gran is disappointed.

"Maybe Reverend Mother is busy praying that you have more good days," I say to cheer her up.

Today, Holy Saturday, is not a good day. Kathy has a cold, the March weather is lousy, and Gran realizes that tomorrow is Easter only when she sees the cake. Every Easter, Mother bakes a white cake in the shape of a lamb for Reverend Mother. This year she has gone to a lot of trouble. The lamb has a woolly coat made out of coconut frosting and it lies in a nest of green crystalized sugar.

"I've phoned the convent to say you're coming," she tells me as she wraps the lamb in wax paper.

"But it's snowing and Easter's not till tomorrow."

"A little spring snow won't hurt you." She places the cake in a shoe box stuffed with paper towels.

"Today is a good day for Reverend Mother," she says, and then for the zillionth time reminds me to carry the box with both hands, mind my manners, and a lot of other stuff. I go to the bathroom.

Mrs. Walkowicz waves to me from the door of the deli, but I don't let go of the cake to wave back. Wet snow like gobs of ice cream hangs from the street lamps and melts as soon as it hits the pavement. I'd rather die than face the saint. Without Gran there'll be no way to hide from those white layers of holiness. Across the street I can see that the convent steps have been swept. The brass door plate and bell are pale yellow. I'm tempted to leave the shoe box at the convent door, ring the bell, and run. As I start up the convent steps the sun comes out and the chapel steeple points a blinding finger at God.

"Your mother is always so good to us." Sister Ann's squat figure is waiting in the doorway. "Go into the parlor and I'll remind Reverend Mother."

The parlor is empty and smells of wax and ammonia. The windows and floor shine. Today there is an Easter lily in the center of the table. On the wall opposite the windows Reverend Mother's predecessors peer out of gilt frames into eternity. I walk under them and concentrate on the little brass plaques where the names and dates are engraved. The door opens and Reverend Mother's quick footsteps on the wood floor echo through the room. She does not notice me even when I approach her at the head of the table. Her face is all ridges and hollows and her habit hangs as if there was nothing under it. She must have fasted a lot during Lent, lived like the saints on water and the Holy Eucharist for forty days.

"My mother made this cake for you, Reverend Mother."

She looks down at me, but makes no move to take the box.

"A white cake with shredded coconut frosting." I inch a little closer, my eyes on the silver crucifix that dangles from her rosary. A thin white bone pokes out from the habit. Between it and my hands the box falls and lands with the smack of a wet mop on the floor. Reverend Mother stares at me. Saints can see into a person's soul. Her eyes work like searchlights piercing the smoke of a hidden fire. My soul is black with anger, with sins I've never confessed, never repented of in the darkness of the confessional. I hate her for not saving the baby and my father, for not healing Gran with her prayers. I hold

my breath to keep from screaming at her. My lungs ache
against my ribs. She can hear the vile words pounding
to get out. The blackness is bubbling up in me like hot
tar, my soul is going to explode and splatter against her
spotless veil.

Reverend Mother turns away suddenly. Her face disappears behind the wimple and she circles the room,
waving her arms as if the wide sleeves of her habit were
wings. She stops in front of a window and opens it. A
rush of air lifts her veil. I feel the cold on my face. She is
walking faster and faster, and I'm certain she'll fall with a
crackle of bones on the floor, but instead she floats. As
she glides past me she whispers, "Christ is risen. He is not
here." I bow my head and let the tears come.

"Don't cry, Celia dear. The lamb's neck is broken,
but that won't spoil the taste."

Sister Ann picks up the box and then catches Reverend
Mother by the arm and leads her from the parlor.

"Did you have a nice visit? Did they like the cake?"
Mother calls from the kitchen.

"Fine. They liked it fine."

"You're cold, dear." Gran reaches up from her chair
and rubs one of my hands in both of hers. "How is
Reverend Mother?"

"Fine. She's okay."

"The woman's a saint," I hear Mother say as I rush
out of the room.

In the bathroom I sit on the edge of the tub and eat
a jumbo chocolate bar. I feel like throwing up.

"Mrs. Walkowicz is sunning her fat self on our stoop."
Kathy points down the street and almost drops the
groceries.

"Don't point, and it's not our stoop, it's hers."

Kathy has been bugging me all the way from the supermarket. Now she has stopped in front of the Acropolis Bakery, which has a big red GONE OUT OF BUSINESS sign on the door.

"Hurry up, stupid. Gran's alone and this stuff has to go in the fridge."

Gran is stronger these days, so Mother can leave her and work in the deli where she has learned to make heroes. Sometimes she brings home sausages and potato salad that Mrs. Walkowicz's son lets her have at a discount.

"There's Gran in the doorway and she's got her black hat and white gloves on," Kathy points.

"Beautiful April, girls." Mrs. Walkowicz spreads her large arms to embrace the air.

"Once I catch my breath, Mrs. Walkowicz and I are going to stop in at St. Francis," Gran says.

"We pray, then we have ice cream. Don't worry. I take care of your Gran."

I wait on the stoop as they walk slowly down the street. St. Francis, our parish church, is just around the corner. Gran, limping, is laughing so hard her shoulders shake. Mrs. Walkowicz must be telling one of her stories about the early days in the deli business. She is very proud of the deli and her religion. "I am Armenian Catholic," she told us when we moved in. "When I die, my sons take me to St. Vartan's Cathedral in Manhattan. Beautiful mass in my language. Big choir, incense." Gran agreed it was something wonderful to look forward to.

"How come we don't visit Reverend Mother any more?" Kathy asks, staring at the open fridge with the bag of groceries in her arms.

"Gran can't walk that far yet, stupid."

"I heard Mrs. Walkowicz say her son could drive Gran to the convent anytime."

"Maybe Gran and Reverend Mother are waiting until they both have a good day on the same day."

Kathy is a terrible fibber and therefore never believes what I say. If white lies were mortal sins and she dropped dead right now in the kitchen, she'd go straight to Hell.

"Are you sure you didn't hide in the bathroom and pig out on Reverend Mother's Easter cake?"

"Sure I'm sure."

"Well, I don't get it." Kathy shrugs and pours herself a glass of Koolade from the pitcher Gran left in the fridge for us.

I haven't told anyone what really happened on Holy Saturday. I need to tell someone even if it's only Kathy.

"You have to swear to keep this a secret forever. Go get the prayer book Gran gave you for your First Communion."

She looks kind of scared, but she puts the book on the kitchen table and places her right hand on the white plastic cover made to look like mother-of-pearl.

"I swear in the name of the Father, Son, and Holy Spirit, Amen. What happened?"

"Reverend Mother came into the parlor and went to the head of the table the way she always does."

"Did you remember to curtsy?"

"Don't interrupt. I was really nervous being there alone, but I was polite and held out the shoe box and told her there was a cake in it."

"I'll bet that's when you dropped it."

"No, I didn't drop it, she did. And then she began acting weird."

"Weird?"

"She raced around the parlor flapping her arms." I don't trust Kathy enough to tell her how Reverend Mother looked into my soul.

"Maybe she was trying to fly like in those pictures of saints when they're in ecstasy."

"She wasn't in ecstasy, she was in pain and crazy."

Kathy fingers her prayer book for a minute. Then she pounds the table and yells, "You made the whole thing up because you did drop the cake and that's why Reverend Mother won't see any of us, not even Gran. You're a liar, but I swore not to tell and I won't. Liar, liar!"

She rushes out of the kitchen sobbing and forgets her prayer book on the table.

THERE IS ALWAYS a lot of traffic on Eighty-first Street when Kathy and I get out of school. Today being Friday, the rush hour begins early. Kathy bugs me by hopping on and off the curb into the gutter. At the traffic light on the corner opposite the Home for the Aged I grab her hand. She yanks it away and points across the street.

"Look. There's Reverend Mother."

As far as I can see the sidewalk is empty.

"Up there, stupid," Kathy says and waves. I scan the old brick building with its niches filled with white concrete saints. Their grimy faces are haggard and sad. On the top floor, just under the roof, the windows open out onto a ledge. Reverend Mother is standing on the ledge. If it weren't for the wind catching her veil, she could be one of the statues.

"I'm scared she'll fall," Kathy whispers and takes back my hand as Reverend Mother starts to pace back and forth.

"She won't," I say, but I'm not so sure. It's getting dark and the light from the street barely reaches the ledge.

Pedestrians stop and press around us. Down the block a cop is redirecting traffic. Now the street, cut off by squad cars, is empty.

"What the hell is going on?" someone in the crowd behind us asks.

"Must be one of the old people in the home. Looks like she wants to jump," a man in a sweat shirt answers and pushes in front of me.

"Crazy," his friend says.

I edge away, pulling Kathy with me through the crowd.

"Move on," the cops, waving red light sticks, call over the noise of sirens and patrol car radios, but nobody moves.

"Wow, Mom, here come the firemen," a small boy near us shouts as an enormous fire truck pulls into the street.

The upper part of the building is totally dark now except for a faint light that shines through the open window behind the shadowy figure.

"She looks like a ghost walking on air," Kathy murmurs.

Suddenly floodlights from the fire truck blaze across the brick. The saints pop out of the darkness. Reverend Mother hesitates, and for a moment it looks as if she is going to climb in the window, but then she turns and faces the light. Her jaw bone and chin jut out from the wimple and her silver crucifix swings from her waist. Gray faces press against a lower window. The aged blink and wave. Then a nun pulls down the shade.

"There goes the cherry picker," someone shouts. We

all watch in silence as the ladders unfold from the fire truck and raise the cabin slowly in the shadows behind the floodlights. On the sidewalk below the ledge firemen hold a large circular canvas. Kathy begins to cry but I pay no attention, because I have spotted a policewoman in the open window behind Reverend Mother. She sits on the sill and makes friendly gestures. Reverend Mother moves out of reach, and then she sees the cabin of the cherry picker inching toward her.

"Take it easy, Ma'am," a fireman calls. "Why don't you go back inside?"

She leans over and stares down into the crowd. She is looking for me. Her eyes are getting closer and closer.

"Stop it. Stop!" I shout out all my terror and hate, but she keeps coming in a great leap like someone tossed off a trampoline. The habit puffs out with air. There is nothing under those layers of white, nothing but air and bones.

"What happened?" Kathy sobs into her hands.

"It's okay. The firemen caught her in the canvas."

I AM SWEATING. Behind Mother and me, the aged rattle their rosaries against the pews.

"Kneel down with me," Mother whispers and tugs at my sleeve, but I'm afraid to get closer to the coffin.

Reverend Mother doesn't look dead, doesn't look like the heap of bones I came to see. She lies on her back and holds the silver crucifix firmly against her chest with both hands. The outline of her body shows faintly under the white habit. My father's face in the hospital was twisted and unshaven, the baby's almost purple, but here in the candlelight this face is smooth and soft-looking.

Some saints' bodies don't ever turn to dust. They remain solid and smell of roses. I feel sick to my stomach and begin to shake.

"It's all right, Celia dear," Mother says as we leave the chapel. "Now Reverend Mother is looking down on us from Heaven."

"A BEAUTIFUL DAY." Gran looks out the window from her armchair. "I hope tomorrow will be the same."

Tomorrow is August fifteenth, the feast of the Assumption of the Blessed Virgin, who, because she was without sin, didn't die. She went to Heaven on a cloud. Gran has her heart set on going to mass at St. Francis and has already put her hat and gloves on the night table in her room. I don't think she should go. The doctor has increased the heart medicine, and when Reverend Mother died in April he wouldn't let her go to the funeral. This afternoon the ankle is swollen. She sleeps a lot in her chair so she doesn't notice the heat and deli odors that drift in through the window.

"Don't you want to go out with Kathy?" she asks, and dozes off before hearing me say I'm happy to be here with her.

Kathy has a best friend now and they've gone to the corner where the Police Department has opened a hydrant and put a spray cap on it. I'm too old for that kid stuff.

"Maybe an ice pack on the ankle, Celia dear," Gran says, opening her eyes. "Must bring the swelling down so I can get a shoe on tomorrow."

I wrap the ice pack in a dish towel so it doesn't sweat on her stocking. Even on very bad days she is fussy about her appearance. This morning I helped her fix her hair, which although white is really thick.

"Your father got his fine black hair from me," she often reminds me.

I look at her in the mirror and search for his features, but her face is old and my memory of him has blurred. When I bring the two together, all I see is a stranger, an old man with thick black hair.

"The ice does feel good. Thank you, Celia." She smiles and rests her head on the back of the chair. "I just had a comical dream."

Thanks to Gran's dreams I know a lot about when she was a child at St. Mary's School. I can see Sister Agnes, the principal, "a tiny person as quick as a ferret who always carried a ruler." Gran had a pet ferret named Mischief, and I hope this dream is about him.

"No, but it is about real mischief and it happened in church, yes in church when the little ones were about to make their First Communion. All the parents were there. We older girls—my friend Cecilia and I must have been in the fifth grade—sat in chairs along the wall, and I could see Sister Agnes out on the steps making the children line up single file. She tapped the leader with the ruler, and as the procession began, Cecilia nudged me and whispered, "The wrath of God is at hand. Pass the word." She was always making up crazy things. All the parents turned to watch the little girls in their starched white dresses and veils as they entered the church and blessed themselves at the holy-water font before they came down the aisle. Sister Agnes was at the end of the line, so she couldn't see that when each child made the sign of the cross, terrible black stains appeared on her forehead and dress. Well, as you can imagine, the holy innocents were in tears and the parents were furious. My mother, your great-grandmother, rushed from her pew and called to Sister Agnes, 'Someone poured black ink in the holy water font.' That's when I woke up."

"Oh, Gran, you must know who did it."

She nods and pauses to catch her breath. "I remember very well, because it was my friend Cecilia. She was a devil at that age. No one, least of all poor Sister Agnes, could have guessed she'd grow up to become a Reverend Mother and give all that energy to the sick and the aged."

Gran's voice is weak and she looks pale in the afternoon light.

"I miss my old friend." She closes her eyes and I think she is alseep, but then she adds, "Your mother wanted to name you after her, but your father, may he rest in peace, was determined to call you Sylvia, after me. Finally he agreed to Celia."

I hate my name and always suspected that Reverend Mother had something to do with it.

"I'd rather be Sylvia, Gran."

"Sweet, you're a very sweet child."

The ice pack is beginning to sweat through the towel onto Gran's stocking. She doesn't notice it, but the sight makes me itchy. The heat and noise of kids playing stickball in the street pour in through the window. I wish Gran and I were in some quiet green town like the place she remembers in her dreams. Elm Street, where the Good Humor man parked.

"Gran, do you believe Reverend Mother is a saint in heaven, like St. Anthony and St. Vartan who saved Mrs. Walkowicz's great-grandfather from the Turks?"

"That's for God to know."

"Well, if she is a real saint, she can work miracles, right?"

"Yes, dear, yes, and such a good baby you were." She sighs and rocks back and forth gently.

"Gran, listen, I'm going to pray to Reverend Mother every night, and if she makes you well I'll believe in her and become a nun and take care of all the sick and aged."

Gran smiles, holding me in her dreams. She doesn't see the blackness, the sins I must confess so that the saint in heaven will forgive me and answer my prayers with a miracle.

"Isn't it time for my medicine?" she asks, half opening her eyes.

"Not for two hours yet, Gran. Go back to sleep."

To make sure I don't forget the medicine, I go into the kitchen and put the pills and drops on a tray with a glass of water.

"Mrs. Walkowicz is down there on the stoop," Gran says when I come back to the sitting room. She is wide awake and waving out the window. "Come see. She's wearing that sleeveless house dress."

Gran disapproves of sleeveless. Mrs. Walkowicz's arms are big and white. Her hair is wrapped around her head in thick white braids.

"From up here she looks like a bunch of deli sausages," I say and Gran laughs.

"She's eating ice cream. With your young eyes can you see what kind?"

I lean through the jungle of Gran's spider plants on the fire escape. "Your favorite. Peppermint swirl."

Mrs. Walkowicz looks up and sees me. "I come visit," she calls.

Gran fusses because of her wet stocking and bedroom slippers. After I remove the ice pack, she has me cover her feet and legs with a sheet.

"Won't you be too hot?"

"No. I'm better this way."

She folds the sheet neatly at her waist.

Mrs. Walkowicz is pulling herself up the stairs. I wait on the landing.

"Please go in, Mrs. Walkowicz. I'm just going to get Gran some ice cream. A surprise."

She leans against the stair railing and slaps it. "I forgot. Your Gran and peppermint swirl. Tell my grandson Eddie no charge."

The deli is crowded with wet little kids. Now that Kathy has a best friend, she doesn't know me.

"Is your grandmother all right?" Mother calls from behind the counter where she is about to put a loaf of black bread in the slicer. "You shouldn't leave her alone."

"She's okay. Mrs. Walkowicz is with her."

The damp cool air of the ice cream freezer feels great, but I can't find any peppermint swirl.

"Need help?"

I've seen Eddie Walkowicz in my school. He's a senior and I've never dared speak to him. Now that I have the chance, I hear myself sounding real stupid.

"Peppermint swirl. I can't find any. It comes in a square pink box."

"Yeah, I know." He bends over the freezer and pokes around.

"It's not for me. I'm a chocolate junkie." I hope he'll take his head out of the mist and say, "Me too," but he doesn't. He disappears in the back of the store. My mother is signaling me to hurry upstairs. Kathy is jigging around on the tile floor and pointing me out to her

71

friend, who giggles as if she'd never heard a person in blue jeans and a T-shirt talk to Eddie Walkowicz.

"How much do you want?" Eddie heaves a large carton on the floor next to the freezer and rips it open with his bare hands.

"A pint is plenty. It's for my grandmother."

"Sure, I've seen her and you with my grandmother. Here."

Now I feel super stupid trying to hold the two slippery one-quart boxes. "Thanks, thanks a lot."

"No prob. See you around." He squats down to unpack the rest of the carton.

Halfway up the stairs I call, "Surprise coming up," but I'm really shouting, "Eddie Walkowicz gave me two quarts of peppermint swirl. He said he's seen me with Gran, and we talked."

The apartment door is open and Mrs. Walkowicz is waiting for me, a handkerchief bunched against her mouth. She wraps an arm around my shoulders so hard, I drop one of the quarts.

"I told Mrs. Martin across the hall to call 911," she sobs into the handkerchief, holding onto me as we go into the sitting room.

The sheet now covers all of Gran. Mrs. Walkowicz lifts it. Gran's head tilts onto her left shoulder. Her eyes are closed but her mouth is open in a sloppy way, and that tells me she really is dead. Mrs. Walkowicz kneels down beside the chair. Ice cream is melting through the seams in the box and between my fingers.

"I stay with her and pray," Mrs. Walkowicz says. "You go get your mother. Tell her your Gran die quietly like a happy person." She takes the pink box from me.

Everything

"YOU TAKE AFTER YOUR FATHER. He caught every bug going," Phil Holden Jr.'s mother said whenever he came down with some minor ailment. Then she would point to the photo of a young man with a thin face and thick hair the color of mahogany. The likeness was striking, and since his father had died at the age of twenty-five, Phil Jr. took this as a warning to be careful of his health. He ate green vegetables, cultivated a positive attitude toward life, and was a faithful husband to his wife Martha. Then he met Alice.

He loved Martha and their two children, Phil the third and Martha minor, but his wife, a sturdy jogger on the road of life, took health for granted, whereas Alice shared his awareness of sickness and death.

He wanted his ladies to like each other, to be friends, but Martha was leery of Alice's dark-eyed, fragile beauty. "That woman will be the death of you," was Martha's reaction to his saying, "I need you both." Then she

73

added, "You can't have both. You think everything, including love, is contagious, that it's spread by kisses like the common cold." She gathered the children to her and locked him out of the house.

"YOU LOOK GREEN," his mother remarked the day he and Alice returned from a vacation in Yucatán.

"I must have picked up something in Mexico. Alice has it, too." He collapsed into a string hammock they had bought in an Indian market.

Alice agreed with his mother that he should consult Dr. Wilson, the Holden family doctor who had brought him into the world and seen his father out of it.

Dr. Wilson's waiting room was empty except for Miss Blakely, nurse and Wilson's companion of many years. Through her receptionist's window she waved him into the examining room.

"Well, young Phil, what seems to be the matter?" Wilson popped his stethoscope into his ears.

"Montezuma's revenge, and I'm lovesick for want of my wife and kids," Phil Jr. replied.

"Well, young Phil, what seems to be the matter?" Wilson folded his stethoscope into the breast pocket of his white coat.

Holden got off the table and shouted his symptoms, omitting the lovesickness.

"You take after your father," Wilson mumbled and went to his desk. "These lab reports just came in." He held one sheet close to his face, then tossed it back on the pile of papers and, pointing a blue-veined hand in the direction of Miss Blakely, said, "We'll set up an appointment for you with Dr. Crump. Speak to my nurse on your way out."

"WHAT DID CRUMP SAY?" Alice asked between swallows of Metamucil.

"Nothing. I didn't see him. His nurse sent me to another lab for more tests and told me to come back in a week."

"Just what they told your father," his mother sighed.

CRUMP'S WAITING ROOM was green, a jungle of spiky potted plants and emerald velvet embossed wallpaper. Phil Jr. surveyed Crump's patients seated in chairs ranged against the wall. Some of the males were bald as doorknobs. A few of the women wore fake fur hats pulled down over their ears. A couple of girls had short layered hair cuts.

"Green, the color of hope," Phil Jr. said to the sallow young woman seated between him and a towering rubber plant.

"Go ahead and hope. You've got plenty to lose." She glared at his thick mahogany hair.

A door opened and a nurse called, "Hope."

As the sallow girl followed the nurse into the inner office, Phil Jr. noted that she had a tricky short hair cut that didn't quite conceal the bald spots.

An older man in faded army fatigues sat down in her chair.

"You see 'em go in but you don't see 'em come out," he said.

"How is that?" Phil Jr. asked out of courtesy. There was no one in the room he particularly wanted to see again.

"After they get the word, they leave by the back door. Some freak out, and you gotta sympathize. Good health is everything. Without it you got nothing." He pushed the red plastic cap with the perforated crown to the back of his head and added that his health was okay. He had just come for a free flu shot from Crump, his son-in-law.

"WHAT DID CRUMP SAY?" Alice asked, rising from her sickbed.

"It's my blood. He gives me six months. I've prepaid for the funeral and the plot."

When Alice freaked out and fell to the floor in a faint, Phil Jr. called Dr. Wilson.

"Get over here. Alice is comatose."

"Call Crump. He's the oncologist."

"I'm the one with cancer, you fool. Alice is sick. Get over here."

"I don't make house calls."

Phil Jr. nursed Alice through the night. In the morning she opened her eyes and asked, "What did you say when Crump said what he said?"

"I told him to stuff his chemo and radiation. I plan to go out with my own hair on."

"I love you," Alice said.

They agreed not to tell his mother the bad news. It would only worry her.

"YOU'RE LOOKING BETTER every day," his mother remarked whenever she stopped by to help take care of Alice, who wasn't looking well.

"Rosier and rosier," Alice marveled.

"I'm so much better, I'm going to run for president,"

Phil Jr. announced one morning as he set a tray of milktoast and herbal tea in front of Alice.

"People won't vote for a dying candidate," she cautioned, but he didn't hear her. He was busy banging together a platform of compassion: a hospice in every hamlet, and strong family values.

When Alice mentioned that the Holden family image wasn't all that great since Martha had sued for divorce, he replied, "Don't worry. I'll use my kids, Phil Holden the third and Martha minor, in the campaign."

"You'll have to kidnap them. Your ex will never let you borrow them."

DURING THE DIVORCE PROCEEDINGS, Martha threatened to accuse him of child molestation unless he gave up all custody rights.

"Try dialogue," his mother and campaign manager suggested.

He dialed his old number.

"This is Phil Holden the third," a six-year-old answered.

"And this is your father, Phil Holden the second. I want your vote so I can go to the White House."

"When are you coming home to this house, Daddy?"

"When I'm president and feel good about myself."

"I miss you."

"I miss you, too," Martha minor chirped in the background.

"This conversation is making me feel so rotten, I'll never make it to the White House."

"Phil, leave the children alone," his ex shouted into the phone.

"I love them. You'll be sorry when I'm president."
He hung up.

WHEN ALICE had recovered sufficiently to get out of
bed, he bundled her into the car and took her to see
Dr. Wilson, who advised her to take it easy and come
back in three weeks. That night she died in her sleep.
Aneurysm, embolism, something quiet, something lethal.
At graveside, he was certain that everyone was making
a gigantic mistake.

"Hold it, you guys," he yelled at the undertaker's men
and stood astride the grave to keep them from lowering
the coffin. "This is my plot and that's my box paid for
six months ago. You can't bury it without me."

Friends dragged him away.

"I DIDN'T KNOW you were supposed to be dead by now,"
his mother said with a worried look.

"I didn't want to worry you, so I didn't tell you."

"Thoughtful, like your father, but neither of us need
worry now. Dr. Wilson phoned while you were out.
Another Phil Holden, not a junior, died today on sched-
ule. There was a mix-up in the lab reports. Your blood
is fine."

He went to the phone and called Wilson, who said,
"Well, young Phil, you have good blood."

"I also have my father's Army revolver and I do make
house calls, Doc."

MARTHA, PHIL THE THIRD, and Martha minor attended
the trial and listened tearfully as he was charged with

murder. In a press interview Martha said he was a sensitive, compassionate person and would make an excellent president. His mother said he took after his father.

The jury acquitted him on grounds of temporary insanity. Everyone in the courtroom cheered, and the press took a picture of the Holden family reunited at last. Martha invited him to come for supper after he finished his talk show appearances that evening.

"You look terrible, Daddy," Martha minor said when she met him at the door.

"Bad chest cold. That lady juror in the big hat had it. I get everything," he wheezed, keeping his distance to avoid passing the bug along.

"Give the children a hug and don't worry. They take after me," Martha called from the kitchen.

After hugging the children, he dozed in the large desk chair until Martha brought him a plate of greens and a glass of carrot juice.

"I have everything now," he said, and then, heedless of the chest pains, he kissed her and died right there at the desk in the Oval office.

Grass

"BORING, SUMMER IS BORING," my younger sister Jennie sighed, dangling her legs over the edge of the tree house. "Sun is boring. Even Justine melting into the arms of Nigel under the moonlit portico of her New Orleans mansion is boring."

"That's because you've already read that trashy book twice."

"You don't seem to be able to get through *Jane Eyre* once."

I had to admit that in spite of my determination to finish all my required summer reading early, I was stuck in the middle of *Jane Eyre*, the first book on the list.

"Summer vacation without Bobby is boring. I'll bet he's forgotten all about the tree house," I said without believing it.

Our brother had always loved the tree house. After

Father died, he was the one who replaced the broken rungs on the ladder and made sure the railings were secure. Every summer vacation the three of us spent hours in the tree house. Bobby would lie on his back, look up through the layers of green into the sky, and dream. His dreams were much more exciting than Justine's adventures, and when he said that one day he would take over the land we had to lease to Uncle Horace and farm it himself, we believed him.

"Since he got his driver's license, all he thinks of is driving around like he was Mario Amato in his Bugatti pursuing Justine," Jennie complained.

Although our brother with his dark eyes and hair was as handsome as Justine's lover, I couldn't transform his old pickup into a Bugatti. But I agreed. "All he thinks of is driving and grass."

Bobby was famous for grass. Thanks to him, our lawn had always been the most beautiful one on Torrey Road. He adjusted the blades of the mower so they didn't cut too close to the roots. He knew what seed mixture and fertilizer did best where. Since Bobby had such a way with grass, he found plenty of summer work from city people who were buying up the farms around Clinton. He made good money, because the first thing the city people wanted was acres and acres of lawn around the old frame houses.

"That brother of yours is a real worker," Mother would tell us. "He'll make a fine farmer some day. For now we have to watch every penny."

That meant eating the same old macaroni and cheese casseroles, chicken and eggs from Uncle Horace, and tons of vegetables from Mother's garden. Occasionally she gave in to Jennie and me and took us to Paul's Pizza in Clinton where they had family specials. Otherwise we always ate at home.

"I pine for pizza right this minute, while Justine and Nigel dine on grouse by candlelight," Jennie said, opening a package of Twinkies we had brought from the house.

I went back to Jane, who was cold and hungry.

"Bobby ought to make lots of money this summer cutting you-know-whose grass," Jennie giggled, pulling the book out of my hand. "Let's go spying."

"That brother of yours," Mother said as soon as she saw us walk out of the woods. "If this grass isn't cut soon, it will be nothing but chickweed and dandelions." She paced back and forth on the lawn. Her face was red and the faded denim skirt she wore for working in the vegetable garden was streaked with mud.

"Do you girls have any idea where he went?"

"Not a clue." I crossed my fingers. At the beginning of the summer, Jennie and I had followed on our bikes the pickup's trail of dust and discovered it always led to the same driveway.

"You're sure?" Mother insisted.

Jennie is a blabber. To keep her from telling everything we knew, I volunteered, "Maybe he's working at the Wallaces' this afternoon."

"The Wallaces?"

"Oh, Mother, you know. The people who bought the Hammond farm on Torrey Road."

Mother's Saturday marketing took her in the opposite direction from the Hammond place, but she remembered having passed it once some time ago and seen a lot of New Orleans–style wrought iron being added on to the porch of the farmhouse.

"The Wallaces moved in this spring. The barn, it's

painted yellow with black trim, has been made into a guest house. Mr. Wallace, he's in import-export, comes weekends. Mrs. Wallace does over old houses, according to Harriet Beal's mother, who works for Clinton Realty."

"That will do, Jennie. We don't gossip about our neighbors. Those peas I left on the kitchen table should be shelled so we can have them for supper. If Bobby shows up, remind him the lawn needs mowing. I'll be in the garden."

"You stupid asshole. You almost spoiled everything," I snarled at Jennie as we biked along Torrey Road.

"You shouldn't have mentioned the Wallaces. If she ever sees what they've done to the Hammond place, she'll have a zillion fits."

"She never wastes gas. The Hammond place is out of her way," I answered in self-defense, but I knew Jennie was right. Mother would not only hate the yellow barn. She would hate the Wallaces who had ploughed under Mrs. Hammond's vegetable garden and all the flower beds.

When we reached our hiding place, a clump of overgrown lilac bushes on the edge of the road, we crawled in and pulled our bikes after us.

"Wow, look. If Mother ever sees that, she'll skin Bobby alive," I whispered.

In front of the Wallace house the freshly mowed lawn glistened under a spray of whirling sprinklers. Mary Beth Wallace stood at the bottom of the porch steps and watched Bobby haul the sprinkler hoses in position so that the water would be evenly distributed.

"She's almost as beautiful as Justine," Jennie said.

Mary Beth, in a green sleeveless dress, her amber hair to her shoulders, seemed to float in the sunlit mist that rose from the grass. Suddenly a small pale woman in a pink pants suit appeared on the porch. Mrs. Wallace never came out of the house except to get in her white Honda. Now she hesitated on the porch and, leaning over the wrought iron railing, called, "I'm in a rush, dear."

"Okay, Mrs. Wallace, just a minute." Bobby disappeared around the far side of the house.

The sprinklers slowed into lazy circles and then stopped, leaving the grass as smooth and glossy as wet fur.

"Bye, darling," Mrs. Wallace said, passing Mary Beth on the porch steps.

As she hurried along the driveway to her car, her high heels sank into the gravel, so that she pranced like a hackney pony we had once seen at the county fair horse show.

"I'll bet she's going to town to get something super like steak and mud pie for supper," Jennie mused.

"Stop thinking with your stomach and watch."

We peered through the dust kicked up by Mrs. Wallace's Honda. Bobby and Mary Beth sat on the porch steps. He stroked her golden hair. She rested her cheek against his. They kissed. Then she rested her cheek against his, and he stroked her golden hair.

"This is boring, and the gnats are biting. Let's go." I started to crawl out of the bushes, but Jennie pulled me back.

A silver blue Chrysler roared past us, turned into the driveway, and skidded to a stop in front of the house.

"There's my girl," Mr. Wallace shouted as he got out of the car and held out his long arms.

Mary Beth ran to him.

"Place looks terrific, Bob," he boomed. "Glad we got

rid of that iris bed. After they bloom, you've got nothing but spiky leaves all summer long."

"Sure, Mr. Wallace." Bobby laughed. "Over there, where you had me take down those apple trees, the grass is coming along great."

Mr. Wallace put one arm around Mary Beth's waist and the other around Bobby's shoulder. Together they began to walk across the lawn.

Spying on them inspecting new grass was no thrill, and we were about to push our bikes out of the bushes when we heard a car coming. In fact, there were two cars, Mrs. Wallace's white Honda followed by Mother's blue Chevy. They lined up behind Mr. Wallace's Chrysler and Mary Beth's Subaru.

"Hello, Robert. Go on with your work." Mother waved to Bobby. Getting out of the Chevy, she went to introduce herself to Mrs. Wallace, who teetered on one foot in the driveway while she removed a shoe. A trickle of gravel fell through the open toe.

Mr. Wallace and Mary Beth joined them, leaving Bobby standing like a stump on the edge of the lawn.

"Mother looks terrific." I nudged Jennie.

The white linen dress with a row of tiny mother-of-pearl buttons down the front had been a present from Father. She washed it spring and fall to keep the linen from turning yellow, and then put it away wrapped in tissue paper.

"I see you have made a few changes," Mother said, looking at the grillwork on the porch.

"We've upscaled the old place. The girl here always wanted to live in a farmhouse."

Mr. Wallace squeezed Mary Beth's hand. She smiled a pearly smile. Mother handed Mrs. Wallace a basket of garden vegetables. Mrs. Wallace looked surprised.

"Love it," Mr. Wallace said, and then they all went into the house to admire the improvements.

THAT EVENING AT SUPPER—macaroni and cheese and, since the peas never got shelled, baked acorn squash—Mother was in a fury.

"Bobby, you have only tomorrow to get our lawn in shape. I invited the Wallaces for Sunday lunch."

I couldn't believe it. We never had guests.

"Will you make something fantastic?" Jennie asked. But Mother's mind was on grass.

"I want the lawn mowed, weeded, edges trimmed. Mr. and Mrs. Wallace can't come, but Mary Beth will be with us."

Bobby left the table and dashed out the back door. It was already dark outside, but from the kitchen window I could see his white T-shirt bobbing up and down as he struggled to get the mower going. Finally the motor sputtered and the machine moved. But the tall grass was heavy with dew. After a few minutes the mower quit. Bobby, a flashlight in one hand and a wrench in the other, was still working on it when Jennie and I went to bed.

"THE LAWN LOOKS as if Uncle Horace's heifers had chewed the edges," Mother said at breakfast.

Since it was pouring rain, mowing was impossible. Bobby had vanished.

Mother pounced on us. "I want you girls to wax the kitchen floor and dust the photographs on the shelf over the fireplace. At least the inside of the house will look decent for lunch tomorrow."

"We could eat in the dining room," I suggested.

"We'll eat in the kitchen the way we always do," she answered, and left for her Saturday marketing and bargain hunting in Clinton.

"And we'll have chicken the way we always do." Jennie flipped the feather duster at the mantelpiece. "Hey, look at this."

Mother always dusted the photographs and postcards over the fireplace herself: pictures of her and Father in front of the Eiffel Tower, the Colosseum, and other places they had visited on their honeymoon. We were so used to seeing these faded souvenirs, we had never noticed what appeared to be a handwritten document in a brown frame. Jennie lifted it off the shelf and placed it on the kitchen table. Under the heading "Maxime's" we read columns of words only a few of which we recognized. We had never eaten *Quenelles saumon fumé ris de veau*, but in mirrored alcoves under the twinkling light of crystal chandeliers we had savored them with Justine. However, I couldn't visualize the young farmer and his bride dining in Paris. The man in the photographs had no connection with my hazy memory of my dying father. The woman did look something like Mother, but it had never occurred to me that she, whose cooking was so boringly basic, might have tasted caviar and drunk champagne.

"Fourteen desserts." Jennie ran her finger down the list. Then we put the menu back in its place.

BY MIDMORNING the skies cleared. With our books and a supply of cookies we dashed down the porch steps and headed for the woods.

"If Bobby makes a roof for the tree house like he promised, we can camp out even in bad weather," Jennie said, stopping to rewrap *Flames of Ecstasy* and the Fig Newtons in Saran.

I walked on. The woods were quiet except for the sound of rain dripping onto layers of pine needles. Some distance ahead, the trunk of the beech, slick with rain, was visible, but the tree house was hidden in the dense foliage of its upper branches.

"I hear something," Jennie whispered behind me. "Something in the tree house."

"Squirrels. They're looking for crumbs."

"Those aren't squirrel sounds," Jennie insisted.

After a few more steps, I agreed. "Voices. Bobby and Mary Beth are up there."

Streaks of gold and black hair showed through the slatted sideboards.

"They're embracing passionately." Jennie pulled me behind a rock, and we crouched down side by side.

"Sounds more like wrestling. And now she's crying."

"In *Flames of Ecstasy*, Justine weeps softly in Guy d'Arblay's arms."

"How come?"

"Read the book, stupid. Bobby and Mary Beth are madly in love."

Bobby's voice grew louder. I couldn't make out the words, but he sounded mad. I didn't want to spy on them any more, and it was starting to rain again.

"Maybe they'll elope tonight under cover of darkness," Jennie said as we left the woods.

"Mother will never forgive Bobby."

"Mother likes Mary Beth. She's invited her to lunch."

Underfoot, the lawn was like a shaggy sponge.

"Mother won't forgive Mary Beth," I said, brushing soggy dandelion fuzz off my legs.

MOTHER WAS SUPER POLITE and stiff as a stick when Mary Beth arrived with Bobby at noon on Sunday. He had spent all morning repairing the mower and had made just one trip the length of the lawn when Mother, who had been silent all morning except to remind Jennie and me to set an extra place at the table, went out on the porch and told him to stop mowing.

"It's time for you to get cleaned up and go for Mary Beth. You can take my car," she said in a tight voice.

Jennie and I were tearing romaine and Boston lettuce leaves into a wooden bowl when Mary Beth, golden in a dress the color of her hair, walked into the kitchen and said in her wispy voice, "What a wonderful house, Mrs. Holt. Have you always lived here?"

"Always, and some day Bobby will be running the farm like his father and grandfather," Mother replied briskly and opened the oven to prick the chicken skin with a fork.

Bobby led Mary Beth by the hand over to the kitchen window and pointed to the vegetable garden.

"Those tall plants with the yellow blossoms, what kind of flower is that?" Mary Beth asked Mother.

"Tomatoes. Do sit down. Lunch is ready."

Mary Beth sat next to Bobby.

"You don't know beans about gardening," he said, and they both laughed.

At the head of the table Mother served, and Jennie and I passed the plates. Mary Beth was very impressed by the fact that we grew most of our food. She had a colossal appetite, bigger than Bobby's, bigger even than Jennie's, and an equally enormous curiosity about cooking. How had mother made the stuffing, braised the celery? What herbs had she used besides tarragon? Mary Beth was eager to talk, but Mother's response was meager, and it reminded me of times when I was little and would ask, "Do you love me best?" She would stop weeding or mending and hold out her fist. As I pulled out one finger at a time, she answered, "I love you (thumb) Jennie (forefinger) Bobby (middle)." Then she would curl us back into her palm. One time before she could do so, I pulled at the remaining two fingers, but they stuck so tightly together, I couldn't budge them. When Jennie, who was watching, gurgled "Mommy Daddy," Mother withdrew her hand and we never played the game again.

Now in answer to Mary Beth's questions, Mother shrugged and said, "This is just a simple country meal."

"It doesn't sound simple to prepare. I do love to eat, but I know nothing about cooking."

"How come?" Jennie, whose role model was a combination of Justine and Julia Child, asked.

"I never had a chance to learn."

"How come?"

"We always ate out."

The words hung over the table, and then Jennie grabbed them. "Always, every single meal including breakfast?"

"Especially breakfast. In Vienna there was a café near our pension where I used to gorge on coffee with chocolate and whipped cream. In Rome my father found this espresso bar."

The smile on Mother's face hardened, and Bobby

stared at his water glass, but Mary Beth, encouraged by Jennie's and my questions, described meal after meal, some eaten on the run at odd hours, others consumed at leisure in elegant restaurants. While Mother was feeding us boring healthy fare, the Wallaces were eating out across Europe.

"What about school?" I asked, aware from my reading in *Jane Eyre* that life was a grimly serious matter.

"For a time, when my father was in Brazil, they sent me to school in Switzerland. It was cold in the mountains, and since I knew hardly any French, just enough to read a menu, I couldn't talk. It was terribly lonely. When I told the headmistress that I was homesick for Harry's Bar, she said I was a bad influence and that my parents were gypsies."

Mary Beth's voice died away as if smothered in snow.

"Have some more chicken," I said, thinking of poor homeless Jane.

"I already had seconds," Mary Beth blushed.

"Have a Brownie made by me." Jennie passed the plate, and Mother began spooning apple sauce from a large bowl into smaller bowls.

"I'm really going to miss living here," Mary Beth sighed.

Jennie's elbow jabbed my ribs. The serving spoon slid from Mother's hand into the apple sauce.

"You're leaving us?" Mother asked.

"Yes, it's just been decided. New York for a while, and then, if my father gets the dealership, we'll go to Paris."

"When do you go?" Mother resumed serving and added an extra spoonful of apple sauce to Mary Beth's bowl.

"Tonight. A friend of my mother's—he's in insurance—is buying the house and everything in it."

"Certainly simplifies packing."

Mother looked around the room at the open shelves piled with generations of cake pans, griddles, steamers, a duck press. I had never seen her use any of them.

For a while nobody said anything. Mary Beth gazed into Bobby's eyes. Bobby gazed into Mary Beth's eyes. Jennie crumbled her Brownie on the tablecloth and picked out the nuts. Normally Mother would have ordered her to mind her table manners, but now she relaxed and seemed content to sit back and watch us eat.

Suddenly Jennie jumped up, took the menu from the mantelpiece and handed it to Mary Beth, saying, "My parents went to Paris on their honeymoon."

Mary Beth brightened the moment she saw it. "Maxime's. Isn't it super, Mrs. Holt?"

Mother nodded and took a sip of water. When we were little, she had shown us the photos of Father, but beyond saying, "We had a wonderful time," she had never talked about Europe and we had never bothered to ask.

With Bobby glancing over her shoulder, Mary Beth held the menu in front of her with both hands and studied it.

"What did you order, Mrs. Holt? I hope you chose my favorites." She fixed her golden eyes on Mother.

"I don't remember," Mother answered, flustered, as if hoarding some great secret.

"What did you have for dessert?" Jennie asked.

"A soufflé called Grand Marnier," Mother mumbled.

"Not my favorite," Mary Beth said, looking disappointed. She handed Mother the menu and asked, "What did your husband have?"

We all stared hard at Mother.

Bobby leaned his arms on the table. "What did Father eat?"

Mother fidgeted with her napkin while we waited in silence.

"First we drank cassis. The evening was warm. Your father was thirsty. He had two glasses, and after I finished mine, I sipped some of his." She swallowed as if she could still taste it.

I wanted to ask what cassis was made of, but didn't, afraid Mother would stop remembering. But Mary Beth was so anxious to get to the meal, she burst out, "And did you have the lobster parfait?"

Mother smiled. "No, like good tourists we had snails, which neither of us much enjoyed. I wish we had known about your favorite. I do recall lobster sauce with the quenelles."

"And then?"

"Coq au vin. Braised chicken with red wine brandy, minced salt pork. Delicious."

Jennie exploded, "Mother, you didn't order boring chicken, did you?"

Mother paid no attention. She was drinking champagne, strolling along the Seine with Father. We weren't there. She wore a dress with pearl buttons. She and Father talked and talked. She breakfasted on fraises du bois and brioche. She was happy.

Bobby, Jennie, and I listened and gaped as she asked, "Remember an Italian *gelateria* on the Left Bank? Open all night."

Yes, Mary Beth remembered. She had been there and

to all those other delicious places. Then she sobbed, "We always ate out," and buried her face in Bobby's shoulder.

He stroked her hair.

"Jennie, put some of your brownies in a doggy bag. Mary Beth can enjoy them while she's packing," Mother said.

AFTER BOBBY AND MARY BETH LEFT in Mother's Chevy, Mother changed into her denims, and although she usually rested on Sunday she disappeared beyond the sweet corn at the far end of the vegetable garden. When she returned to the house shortly before supper time, she looked tired and troubled.

"Bobby back yet?"

"Not yet," I said and suspected we were both worried about the same thing. Bobby might not come back at all. Those Wallaces—Mrs. with her "Bobby darling" and Mr. with his "Terrific, Bob" and Mary Beth with her golden tears—would lure him away from us forever.

"Let's eat," Jennie said, opening the fridge.

"No, we'll wait for your brother."

Mother stood at the window and watched for her Chevy on Torrey Road. While she had her back turned to us, Jennie, seated opposite me at the kitchen table, signaled for me to read her lips.

"Eloped, they have eloped."

I shook my head. Bobby belonged here. If Mary Beth really loved him, she would stay and learn to cook and garden while Bobby farmed. Mother would be happy to have someone to talk to besides Jennie, who babbled nonsense, and me, who couldn't get through *Jane Eyre*.

"How about a snack, snails, lobster parfait, some damp Fig Newtons, while we're waiting?" Jennie pleaded.

Mother left the window, put a pitcher of iced tea with fresh mint on the table, and sat down beside us.

"Maybe someday I'll get a nice chicken from Uncle Horace and make coq au vin."

"Someday when?"

"Be quiet. Listen."

The loud steady chugging of a motor filled the silence.

"Bobby's home." She rushed onto the porch.

In the dusk the lawn looked like a shallow lake, its surface rough with tall weeds.

"Be ready with those rakes, you two," Mother shouted at us over the noise of the motor. Bobby, stripped to the waist, was hunched over the mower like a jockey asking for speed.

Grass spun off the blades in a steady stream, and the evening air smelled so sweet and cool, I opened my mouth to taste it while Jennie and I hurried behind the machine.

Raking the clippings into mounds was hard work. The grass, still wet from the rain, was sticky. It balled up in the teeth of the rakes and coated our bare legs and hands.

Bobby had just finished the last stretch of lawn down along Torrey Road when a car pulled over, catching the three of us in its headlights. Bobby stopped the mower, planted his feet on the ground, and shielded his eyes with one hand.

"You do a great job even in the dark," Mary Beth said, leaning out the car window.

"Thanks. You're on your way?"

"Yes." She opened the car door.

As he walked over and got in beside her, Jennie and I scurried out of range of the headlights.

"This is it. Now they'll embrace passionately and drive

away into the night," Jennie whispered as we huddled in the shadows on the porch steps.

"Maybe if they embrace passionately, she'll decide to stay here with us."

"Sure, and eat macaroni and cheese when she could be having lobster parfait at Maxime's."

The Subaru headlights dimmed. Inside the car, two profiles faced each other in the faint light of the dash.

"What are you girls up to there?" Mother called from the dark porch.

"Nothing."

The porch lights came on, and she hurried down the steps, Bobby's weed sprayer slung over her shoulder. Jennie and I grabbed our rakes and ran ahead of her. We were supposed to rake the clippings so she could get at the roots of the weeds.

She was in a frenzy, muttering, "Take that, and that," and, "Come on, girls, don't dawdle."

We stepped aside for fear of getting sprayed as she zigged and zagged. Then, shouting at the weeds, she went parallel to the road, to where the car was parked.

"Mother, be careful with that stuff, or you'll kill the grass," Bobby called, jumping out of the Subaru.

She answered that she knew what she was doing and he had better help with the raking before the clippings rotted and killed the grass underneath.

We knew that couldn't happen overnight, but Mother was taking no chances.

Bobby raced in circles, flailing the cut grass with wide sweeps of the rake, until the air was alive with green spirals whirling like dust devils.

"You're supposed to make piles," I said, pointing to the neat mounds of clippings Jennie and I had prepared for the compost heap.

He charged us, laughing and humming, "Waves, cyclones, blizzards of grass," as our piles disintegrated.

Jennie and I collapsed on the lawn and watched Bobby and Mother. She continued to pursue dandelions and burdock, even though the sprayer had run out of weed killer and did nothing but wheeze. Bobby chased after her, complaining that she was destroying new growth, ruining his grass worse than moles or grubs or black ants. When he caught up with her, he took hold of her arm. She dropped the sprayer, and for a minute they stood side by side, too breathless to speak. Bobby's hair and clothing were so coated with grass, he looked as if he had grown a green pelt.

"Goodbye," Mary Beth called from the road.

Bobby waved, but she gunned the Subaru into high gear and I doubt if she saw him.

"She must think we're crazy," Jennie said when we all walked toward the house together.

Halfway up, Mother turned and looked back. By now the lawn and road were one continuous shadow. In the pasture beyond, a black-and-white heifer slowly lowered her head into tall clover.

"Grass isn't easy," Mother said, and we went in to supper: leftover chicken and salad.

Saying Something

WE ARE ACCUSTOMED to winter, to the isolation and silence that settles on this town, wedged as it is between hills and sea. The snow comes early, the flakes at first as light and soft as milkweed floss. When the temperature drops, crystals sting the cheeks and hiss on the windowpanes like bluebottles in summer. Once the air clears, the sky and sea are an unbroken neon blue devoid of shading. Our breath mists before our eyes as we watch the barrier of ice close the mouth of the harbor. Fed by incoming tides, the glassy massif rises out of its own reflection, an ice city of high walls and luminous towers. Facing it across the harbor, our town huddles in the drifts, and we, like small burrowing creatures, scurry from door to door in the glare of this glacial skyline. The ice city is silent. No chimes ring from its towers.

The canyons release no echoes, and the silvery water of the harbor is a mirror without resonance.

The only sound we hear throughout the winter is that of our own voices, buzzing under snowladen roofs, halloing cheerfully back and forth along Main Street. We are a sociable, garrulous community of fishermen and loggers, and in the evenings everyone gathers at Jake's Beer and Burger to talk. Like any small town, we have our quota of sharp tongues, but mostly the conversation about family, jobs, young loves, and old alliances is good-natured and without surprises. Everything that can be said on such matters has been repeated many times over, and since a number of us are kin, even the names of the newborn, the dying, and the dead tend to be the same. The talk around the tavern tables flows easily. No one expects to hear anything new; no one hesitates to retell an old story. The enclosing silence must be filled, the isolation overbridged with rumors, arguments, speculations, and, as the nights lengthen, with counter-rumors, counter-arguments, counter-speculations.

One winter, the cold was more severe than any remembered. The milky floes congealed and compacted to ominous heights, imprisoning the harbor and stopping just short of the wharf. From the shore we peered up at the ice city. Through its lofty arcades, frigid drafts swept down on the town and turned the snow on our roofs hard and slick as porcelain, while in the hills birches, white on white, trembled in their ice-glazed skin. On moonless nights the sky seemed to retreat to some remote darkness, leaving the towers to thrust their spires into the void.

We continued to meet at Jake's as the winter took its toll: a storage shed collapsed, damaging several boats, a rock slide closed the road to the south. The talk around the tavern tables grew more and more trivial and repetitious. The discussion, one evening, passed from the weather to the Sheldons' new baby. The infant, born prematurely and at home, road conditions making the drive to the hospital impossible, was not certain to live, but the focus of attention was on the pros and cons of parents' rumored intention to name the child Sheldon Sheldon. All of a sudden old Jeff Galt, who always sat off in a corner drinking alone, stood up and shouted, "Say somethin', say somethin'. You're all stiffs." We tried to draw him into the conversation, but he only grew angrier. "Ya say nothin' and ya are nothin', just stiffs."

Young Jeff finally quieted him down, but the outburst was disturbing. A tacit agreement of long standing had been challenged. Talking about nothing had always been our way of talking about things, things that if said openly would leave us with nothing more to say. After Galt's interruption we went home early. The next morning, when we stepped outdoors, we heard a silence experienced only in nightmares: the soundless moment of an ambush, of a fall into an abyss. As we greeted neighbors, our words froze in the mist of our breath. They echoed in our heads, but no sound passed our lips. After the initial shock, we resumed our daytime chores of checking the boats, splitting firewood, and in the evenings we met as usual at Jake's. A few enterprising souls devised a sign language, but it served for only the most rudimentary communication, such as, "Two beers." Nevertheless, by force of habit we sat conversing, albeit silently. In fact, as time passed, we enjoyed a feeling of release from the old constraints. There was no need to withhold secrets or repeat stale gossip, and so we talked about what we had been talking about for years but not saying.

One evening, we had just gathered at the bar and were signaling our orders, when we heard a rumbling like prolonged thunder. Rushing to the windows, we saw in the starlight that always played above the ice city one of the towers vibrating. The spire toppled first, and then tier after tier crashed into the darkness. The sudden avalanche of sound was awesome. We felt an urgent desire to talk, to hear and be heard, but all we could do was gape at one another, mouthing like fish.

The next morning, we rushed to the shore of the harbor. Against a sky seared white by a fiery sun, the ice city shone in all its splendor. But the tower, in falling, had sheared a crevice in the massif. The fishermen among us gesticulated excitedly and pointed to the sea current that worked its way in and out of the fissure. Little tongues of foam licked the ice. Suddenly, above the skyline we saw a blaze of colors, as if a rainbow had shattered and was now spinning in a multitude of fragments across the face of the sun. Birds, brilliantly plumed tropical birds wheeling in unison, coursed around the frozen turrets and then circled above our heads. Scarlet macaws, purple-black mynas, parrots, crested cockatoos filled the stillness, and in their voices we instantly recognized our own. Everything we had uttered in the frozen silence of winter was suddenly soaring and shrilling in a confusion of beating wings. The tavern rose, drawn in the updraft of joyous release, and there in the sky we heard Mary and Ron Wells talking of love, and Eliza Sheldon, our choir's most beautiful contralto, cursing God and herself for the loss of her baby. "This damn fool's dying. Can't ya see I'm finished?" a white cockateel mimicked Jeff Galt, hoarse and drunk. "Peace, justice, freedom," a fluttering of green and yellow parakeets chimed boisterously while, on the shore, mothers clapped with delight to hear their young rise above the lamentations of the old. The sky reverberated like a gong, blending all the voices into a wild harmony.

Joe Watson stepped out of the crowd and walked onto the wharf. "Tide's turning out," we heard him say, and when we realized that we could actually speak to one another, we began to cheer, grabbing the nearest person, shouting his or her name and our own, all of us babbling like children. "Peg Mike Tony," the birds echoed and disappeared behind the ramparts of the ice city.

"Tide's turning out," Watson repeated, observing the heavy swell that was pulling the massif with it, while under the sun the spires diminished to stunted pillars and the domes, with their supporting walls, shrank to transparent mounds. Then with a tremendous roar the entire mass broke into innumerable little islands that floated and bobbed on the choppy sea like a flock of gulls.

At the tavern that evening nobody said a word. With the harbor open and the crests of the hills steaming as if on fire, we had worked hard all day to repair the winter's damage. Our ears still rang with the noise of cracking and splintering and dripping, as gutters overflowed and every surface exposed to the sun broke through the snow to emerge gaudy and hard-edged. We sat silently, reluctant to hear our own voices or to listen to our neighbors', because all our secrets had been shared. We were hollow and dry as gourds.

"Guess I'll take the old fool home," Jeff Galt announced soberly and left the bar.

We followed. The air, though cold, was alive with the distant rush of streams flowing down from the hills. Under the night sky the sea rolled peacefully, its surface creased and mounded like the palm of a hand brimming with stars.

Match Point

HIS FATHER TAUGHT HIM TENNIS. From the age of eight, for four summers, he has played every Saturday. His father wins. He loses, something he finds increasingly galling, but his father is his father and that's a fact like gravity. Without gravity to draw the stroked ball back to earth there is no game, no winners, no losers.

Today is the final match of the summer. The noon sun is blinding, the court like hot glass.

"Serve 'em up." His father goes into his crouch.

He positions his feet behind the base line. In his left palm the ball feels unpleasantly hairy, like the artichoke heart he tasted just once to please his mother. He prefers the licorice slipperiness of golf balls, but tennis is his father's game and now he must serve. The score, forty-love and match point, unnerves him.

He tosses the ball against the sky, where it hangs for a moment like a dirty moon.

"First service," his father calls as it falls short into the net.

He repeats the toss, angles the racquet for top spin the way his father taught him. The ball grazes the net and dribbles over.

"Let. You get another."

He steadies himself and executes the toss carefully. When the ball descends, he swallows it.

His father rushes to the net. "Ace. I never even saw it."

He leans over, retches in an attempt to regurgitate the ball.

"Your game, set, match," his father shouts.

He slumps against the backstop and shields his eyes with his right hand. His father's round face is spinning further and further away, high into the sun. At last gravity pulls it down next to his.

"You won. What's the matter with you?"

The ball, now under his rib cage, is pressing on his heart. He can't explain that tennis isn't his game.

Ratings

IF ALL THE GIRLS in New Jersey could see Rory Parnell, they would agree with me and every girl in Newark that he is the handsomest, most fun man in the state. A lot of them would wonder what he sees in me. I sometimes wonder.

"Don't fish," my best friend Kathy, who is studying to be a hairstylist, says. "You're not bad."

That about says it. On a scale of one to ten, I give myself a five, maybe even a six with a summer tan in my green strapless bathing suit. Today, while walking back to work after my lunch-hour Jazzercise class, I checked my reflection in the store windows to make certain I'm not falling below a five. My long hair is my best feature. The color, dark mahogany red, is so unusual that women in the supermarket stop and ask me if it's natural.

I squeeze Rory's hand and answer, "It's really a wig."

"Fantastic," Rory chokes with laughter as the embarrassed stranger hurries past us. "You're beautiful. Don't ever cut your hair."

FOR THE PAST TWO WEEKS I've been sick at home. Rory stops by every afternoon after work. Before he arrives, I get out of bed no matter how rotten I feel and do my face, fix my hair, and put on a green velour lounge robe. When Rory admires how well the green goes with mahogany red and kisses me, I feel better immediately.

MY HOSPITAL ROOM is full of flowers from Rory and crazy get-well cards from friends. The nurses eye Rory, gobble him up when he walks past their station. They are sweet to me and very impressed that I am visited every day by the handsomest man on the East Coast.

"You sure are a lucky girl," they say, and I agree that I am lucky to have such a faithful lover in spite of my being thin and sickly.

My doctor has called in a specialist with a narrow face and a beard. When he talks, he chews his words and looks like a llama. I must save my strength for Rory's visits, so I don't ask questions or argue when the llama orders a change of medication.

I feel limp, and my face, hospital white, doesn't rate a five even with makeup.

"With your hair, pale is romantic," Kathy insists.

SHE HELPS ME with my hair, which is full of tangles. More and more clumps come out on the brush. We leaf through the pictures in the stylist book she has brought from the Vogue School of Cosmetology and Hair Design. One photo shows a sexy girl sitting alone on a beach. The caption says, "Vidal Sassoon's Grecian boy look. The carefree you this summer." I decide to go for it in spite of the fact a blizzard is heaping snow outside my window and the Jersey beaches are freezing.

Kathy puts the shorn lengths in a plastic bag and hands me a mirror. On me the Grecian boy rates a four, although the short ends do curl nicely against my head.

"Your hair loves it, Rory will love it," Kathy exclaims.

Rory's smile takes over his face, my room, the hospital floor. The nurses in their white polyester pants-suit uniforms sail through the corridors like weightless astronauts and peek into my room to see the handsomest man in America smile. I toss flowers at them and at Rory, who is standing at the foot of my bed staring at me.

"Fantastic. I love it," he says.

"I hate you, Rory Parnell," I scream and pull the covers over my head as he rides his smile out the window into the snow.

I FEEL RELIEVED and don't fault Rory for not coming anymore. The handsomest man in the world can't be expected to hang around a balding minus-four-and-still-sinking.

The nurses are very crisp, very medical now. When they sponge my face, I sense their disappointment in me. No more candy, flowers, fun chats. They blame me for letting go of Rory. He was their dream hero, the faithful lover, and they figured that I could have held on to him simply by being a three, which is more or less terminal.

The light in the window has turned faintly green, and like the tree outside I am sprouting a few wisps.

"I brought you a present," Kathy says. She sits me in a chair. "Close your eyes and hold out your hands."

Something wonderfully soft and warm, like a drowsy kitten, curls in my hands. Made of my own hair, the wig is light.

"A perfect fit," Kathy admires her work and hands me a mirror.

"Thanks, but no thanks." I push the mirror aside. Although a cold spring wind is rattling the window, I feel summer carefree. When I meet the next handsomest man in the world on some Jersey beach, I won't spend a minute rating myself for him. It's only April, but I know without looking in a mirror that I'm already a six, going up fast.

The Hired Girl

THAT SUMMER the gypsy moths attacked the woods behind our house. In the morning I could see them from my bedroom window, disgusting wormy things swinging among the branches on the long sticky threads they spin from their insides, and at night, even though I pulled the pillow over my head, I could hear the strange noise they made, a sound like drops falling from leaf to leaf after the rain has stopped. "They're crapping, that's what they're doing," my brother Edmund said, but I knew the trees were being eaten alive. By October the maples and oaks had turned into skeletons. Only a big clump of overgrown bayberry bushes at the edge of the woods still had their leaves. My father told me to stop worrying about the trees. Nature would take care of them. At the end of a three-year cycle the gypsy moths would die, actually explode from a virus.

"Nature's disgusting," I said, but both my brothers enjoyed the idea of masses of self-destructing bugs popping like bubble gum in the woods.

Edmund and Willie and I quarreled a lot all that summer. Somehow we always felt angry, and the minute our father left for the farm-supply warehouse in town, we'd gang up viciously two against one. Sometimes the boys would torment me for being a girl. Sometimes one of them would team up with me. If the odd one happened to be Willie, it wasn't much of a battle, because he's the youngest and kind of small for his age. By the end of a hot afternoon the three of us would be kicking and pummeling whoever happened to be within reach. Then someone would shout, "I'll get you next time," and, too exhausted to fight, we'd each go off alone, bruised and aching, to let the anger build to a new pitch.

This was the stage we'd reached one dusty October afternoon. Willie was in the woods hiding behind the bayberry bushes from Edmund, who was lying flat on his belly in the tall grass near the house. I could see both of them from my bedroom window, where I sat sulking and listening to the gypsy moths. Willie had a Canada goose in his arms. Every fall, a flock of wild geese stop to rest and feed in our pond; after a few days they leave. Willie was struggling hard to hug the bird against his chest. He lifted one hand to pat it on the head. The goose honked, flapped, paddled the air, and finally twisted its neck and bit him, first on one cheek and then the other, right on the bone below the eye. Willie let out a yelp. That's when Edmund, who'd been crawling toward the bushes, pulled the trigger. The goose broke free and tumbled down the hill to its mate in the pond. Willie crumpled and disappeared behind the bushes. I heard the front door open and our father call, "I'm home."

Martha, that dumb hired girl who was supposed to keep an eye on us, was waiting for him and primping in front of the hall mirror. That's all she ever did— wiggle and primp—and every afternoon, when he came into the house, she'd pounce on him like a puppy. But this time, hearing the shot, she ran into my room, which is just off the front hall, and began screaming. I knew he'd come rushing in, so I jumped on my bed and closed my eyes tight, not wanting to see him get upset and Martha in her red dress wiggling around him.

As his heavy footsteps crossed the room, Martha bawled, "Edmund's killed William."

My father dashed out, and by the time I got to the window, he was climbing through the bayberry bushes. Martha, still bawling, stood next to me and watched.

"You dumb disgusting girl," I snarled. "We've had lots like you in this house, only prettier than you, and they've all gone."

It was true that since our mother's death, there had been not exactly lots but quite a few Marthas, but none had been as pretty or as young as this one. None had stayed as long.

I must have shocked her, because she stopped crying and stared at me with her dumb blue eyes. Then my father's shouting for her to call Dr. Mason sent her to the kitchen phone.

Lying on the porch sofa, Willie looked like a small dead clown, his face chalky except for a red spot on each cheek.

"Cold water and a wash cloth, Martha," my father bellowed, although she was standing in front of me right next to him.

Edmund had disappeared into the toolshed. Before Martha returned—the dummy brought a plastic pail with a dishrag floating in it—Dr. Mason finished poking Willie in the ribs and was pulling back an eyelid the way they do in the movies to show you that the person is dead. Willie squirmed, sat up, and said his head hurt. Dr. Mason told him that he had hit it on a rock when the goose knocked the wind out of him.

"Powerful birds, Canadas," the doctor said. "And beautiful, but they are wild birds. They don't want you to pet them."

Willie blinked and lay down again.

While my father was walking Dr. Mason to his car, Martha tried to dab Willie's cheeks with the wet rag, but he knocked it out of her hand, and Edmund came squealing out of the toolshed and onto the porch.

"Dumb Martha's got blood all over her dress," he chanted, dancing around her.

She looked down at her skirt, where the water had turned the red to an even brighter crimson. Then she called us a lot of bad names, said that because we were so wicked, God had taken our mother away, and this time He'd punish us but good. The thought of God reaching down like King Kong and plucking up our mother stunned us, and when we didn't answer back, Martha went into the house and slammed the door to her room.

Our father got supper out of the freezer: pizza with sausage and chocolate swirl ice cream. We ate on the porch so Willie could stay quiet, but our father didn't seem to be hungry, and when I asked if I could have his ice cream, he just nodded without looking at me. After we finished eating, he told us there would be no school the next day and perhaps for several days because of a teachers' strike. We would be left on our own until he could find someone to take care of us and the house. He wanted us to help one another instead of fighting all the time.

The next morning, it rained, which seemed to silence the gypsy moths. We couldn't think of anything to do in the house, so we went outdoors and walked down to the pond where the wild geese were swimming silently. As we approached, they roared out of the water, a great thundercloud of dark wings in the wet air. Edmund was in front of Willie and me, and he was the first to see it lying at the edge of the pond, its long neck stretched out toward the water. Willie began to cry, and I did too when I saw the bullet wound.

We dug a hole behind the bayberry bushes. Before we closed the grave, Edmund ran to the toolshed and, I guess to prove to Willie how sorry he was, came back and put the twenty-two down next to the Canada.

"Wild geese have only one mate forever an' ever," Willie sobbed as Edmund and I shoveled dirt into the hole. "They're monogagus."

When we got back to the empty house, we each went to our own room and closed the door.

Recognitions

"I'M GOING TO GROW a beard," she announced at breakfast.

"All right, dear," her parents said, "but don't miss the school bus."

"I'm going to grow a beard," she whispered to Eliza, who was her best friend and the prettiest girl in the sixth grade.

"Dare you," Eliza laughed. "Hey, look at that cute guy who just got on the bus."

"I will grow a beard this summer," she promised herself.

Nobody was impressed until she did. She became the girl with the golden beard, a celebrity. However, people soon got used to the idea, and since her name was Leslie quite a few thought she was a boy and lost interest.

The world was too full of surprises to be shook up

by a beard. In June, Larry, her special boy friend, shaved his head and tattooed the zodiac on his skull. Jeffrey, her baby brother, swallowed a bluebottle fly, and in August a rancher somewhere in Utah claimed his palomino yearling had sprouted a horn and was turning into a unicorn. A blurred picture appeared in the paper, but she was too busy to read the story, which Larry said put the unicorn in the same category as Big Foot.

The beard required more attention than she had bargained for. It caught itself in zippers and collected crumbs. It was hot.

"I'm going to shave the beard," she told her parents at the end of the summer.

"Do that, dear," they said and dashed to a meeting of the zoning board.

She did, and as she stood in front of the mirror she discovered she had grown a new face. It wasn't much more exciting than the old one, a bit paler for having been covered, but there in the glass were cheeks, a chin, jaws, lips, all the necessary parts. It would have to do.

At first people didn't recognize her. She was half glad they didn't. It saved explaining about the beard, but now she had to make an effort to smile and say, "Hello, I'm Leslie." Even then some friends of her parents were surprised and took a minute to smile back with, "Of course, Leslie, you look just like your mother," which was dumb. Anyone could see that Jeffrey was the one who looked like Mother.

But after a while everybody put her name and face together, and in September Larry let his hair grow out. One day after school, they had a Coke and agreed that they were the only people in the world who remembered her old face and the heavens hidden under his hair.

Loving Duds

MY MOM AND DAD are very loving, but if I'd been a car they'd have figured they had a lemon and returned me to the dealer. A photo taken two summers ago when I was thirteen shows me with limp hair, a pug-dog mug. I am seated between my parents on the stoop of our semidetached house faced with fake brick. I don't take after either my Dad, who is bulging out of his postal clerk's shirt, or my Mom, a stocky redhead in a loose-fitting cotton dress and apron. She is clutching a pot holder in one hand; the other rests on my shoulder. Under the photo she has written, "Em, with Griff and me." I'm called Emeline after my Mom. My Dad is Griffin.

All that summer, Mom had been hinting about a baby. I figured she was just imagining how nice it would be to have something around that wasn't a dud like me, and I didn't begin to worry about a little brother or sister until the weekend my Dad moved all his stuff out of the small room next to mine. His bowling trophies, sports magazines, and a steel file cabinet for what he called "important papers" were put in the garage.

I woke up gasping one morning in August. I'm allergic to ragweed, and when the pollen count in New Jersey rises, my respiratory system in White Plains, New York, goes into a spasm. When I went downstairs for breakfast, Mom was leaning over the sink with the tap on. Her shoulders were heaving under her pink and blue housecoat, like she was throwing up. At my sneezing she turned off the water and stood upright. She had been crying.

"We could get a canary," I said. "Who needs a baby waking us up in the middle of the night."

She pulled me against her side. "Don't worry, Em. You're my best girl." I believed her then. Her eyes were as watery and red as mine.

In September I went back to school and came home too tired to worry about anything except Miss Watts, my student advisor, who had figured me as one of the seventh-grade retards.

I was sitting at the kitchen table one afternoon after school, watching Mom water a half-dead ivy planted in a coffee can, when I saw two women with briefcases come to the door. I thought they might be some kind of Avon Lady, except that Mom hurried them into the living room and told me to come when she called.

"This is our daughter, Emeline," she said, and smoothed my hair off my mutt's face when she introduced me.

The ladies smiled, asked some stupid questions about

school. Once they left, Mom explained that they were from the adoption agency and wanted to make sure we were "a good solid family." After that, nothing happened. The room next to mine remained empty. Mom drew the blinds over the window, and when she closed the door behind her, she had a sad, hollow look. Some nights I could hear her sobbing in the kitchen downstairs and my Dad saying, "Don't, Em. After all, we have Em." Mom blubbered even louder, and I lay in bed and felt rotten, because I had wanted the agency to turn us down, and they had. Those ladies with the briefcases and X-ray eyes must have seen I wasn't your ideal solid-family daughter. They had spotted every pimple, crooked tooth, allergy, and "neg ad" toward Miss Watts.

A couple of weeks later, the school nurse sent me home early with swollen glands and a fever. I found Mom tearing around in the room next to mine with the Hoover, so I guessed the baby was back in the picture, but I felt too lousy to care. I woke up late the next morning feeling as if I had been under water for ten years. My parents were chattering like crazy in the next room. Apparently the baby had arrived.

When I stepped into the hall, my Mom pointed to me and said, "Lyn, this is Em."

Baby, hell. The kid was prancing around the room like a monkey, and was she beautiful. Blue eyes, golden curls, white teeth, the whole bit. The sight of her sent my glands ballooning. I went back to bed and decided that the kid had to go.

Lyn was six. According to my Mom, she had always lived with her grandmother. I figured one reason she thought our semidetached split-level was so great was that life in the boonies with Granny hadn't been all that thrilling. Lyn didn't know she was adopted. Dumb-dumb really believed that she had come home.

"When are you going to tell her you're not her mommy?"

"Sometime," Mom answered. She was scrouging around in the refrigerator. Since Lyn's arrival, it was packed with milk. I'm celiac, allergic to milk.

"Sometime when? She's been here four months."

"Your father and I will tell her, once she's used to us and knows how much we love her. So don't you ever say a word."

I could tell she was serious by the way she slammed the refrigerator door and said, "Not one word out of you, Emeline."

"Why can't she go to her own home?"

"Well, because . . . Where did you put the onions?"

"Lyn stuck them in the potato bin." I handed her two onions. "Then why can't she go to relatives?"

Mom had spent the afternoon stalking the January white sales in the shopping center and was late making supper. In her hurry at that moment she probably told me more than she intended. Lyn's father was a "missing person," missing long before her birth. Her mother had given the baby to her mother and gone away to make "a new life."

"Sounds like one of your soaps. Why can't she go live with an aunt?" I'd been thinking about ways to get rid of Lyn for months, and since my parents have lots of family, the aunt solution seemed obvious. But Lyn didn't have any aunts.

"Besides," Mom snapped, "most people won't raise another person's child. Hand me the can opener, dear."

"Then why do we?"

"The can opener, Em. What did you say?"

"Nothing."

"There's your Dad. Go tell him Detective Schmidt wants him to phone about bowling."

All that winter I hated Lyn. I tried feeling sorry for her and being nice to her, but that only made the hate stronger. I hated her dolls. Each one had blonde curls and blue eyes and was named Emmie. The hate was like a horrible scab hardening in my gut. Lyn followed me around, believing every word I said, how I was the most popular girl in my class, how I was going to have the lead in the Christmas play. Sure, Mary with eczema all over her hands holding the Christ Child. Anybody who'd believe that had to be an idiot. Lyn wasn't an idiot, though, she just wanted to believe me. That tempted me more than ever to corner her and let her have it. "You stupid jerk!" I would say. "My parents aren't your Mommy and Daddy and I'm not your sister. You don't belong here. Go find your own mother and father." Maybe she'd run away or collapse before my eyes, but then my parents would be left with only me, and Mom would never stop crying. I kept my mouth shut and my head working.

In March my parents always go to visit Dad's sister in Syracuse, and Aunt Ethel, Mom's not-too-bright sister, comes to stay at our house. When Lyn heard they were going away for two weeks, she panicked.

"Mommy, Daddy, don't leave me." You would have thought they were about to disappear into a black hole.

"You'll love Aunt Ethel," my Mom said.

Aunt Ethel sure loved Lyn. The minute she walked in the door and saw those tearful blue eyes, she gaped and gushed until I thought even Lyn might puke. Probably Aunt Ethel had expected to find another dud.

With my parents away and school out for spring

vacation, Lyn was more of a pest than ever. We were in the garage one rainy afternoon, I horsing around on the mini-tramp, Lyn on her bike, which even with training wheels she couldn't ride.

"Help, Em, help me."

I couldn't catch her, and she slammed into Dad's file cabinet, went down, and the top drawer sprang open. I had always been curious about Dad's important papers, so I stepped over Lyn and looked in the drawer. It contained folders arranged alphabetically, and there in front, under A, a file marked "Adoption" jumped into my hand. Lyn went whimpering into the house to her Aunt Ethel, and I sat down on the mini-tramp to read. The folder contained documents with seals stamped on them, but at the back I found a ruled yellow sheet with notes in Dad's handwriting. The first paragraph set me bouncing on the mini-tramp.

"Lyn Manion, daughter of Gwendolyn, unwed. Child raised by grandmother from birth." The kid was not only adopted, she was a bastard.

Further down the page, Dad had written in red ink: "Bud Schmidt has traced Gwendolyn Manion Carter to 1105 Catron St., Westfield Section of White Plains. He thinks she, being the natural mother, could make trouble if she wants the child."

That night I put myself to sleep humming the beautiful name, "Gwendolyn Manion Carter," and the next day, while we were eating lunch in the kitchen, I announced I was going out to sell raffle tickets. Lyn took the bait.

"Me too, Em, please."

"No, you wouldn't like it. Besides, it might rain."

"Oh, Em, take the child along," Aunt Ethel said, helping Lyn into her rubber boots and the red plastic raincoat I had outgrown. "I can't understand your mother always leaving those tickets for you to sell."

Every spring my Mom takes three books of raffle tickets for the church bazaar, puts them in the kitchen table drawer, and at the last minute sends me around the neighborhood to her friends. They buy hers; she buys theirs. The last minute was still weeks away, but Aunt Ethel didn't know that, and after more fussing with Lyn's hair under the rain hat—"Just like Little Red Riding Hood"—and gripes about my jogging shoes and patched jeans, she let us out the door. I grabbed Lyn by the hand and we just made the express bus that goes across town to Westfield.

"Where we going?" Lyn kept asking, pushing her teddy in my face.

With her, one question always led to another, so I said, "Look out the window and don't bug me."

I had taken this bus before with Mom to go to a mall in Westfield. All she bought were some washcloths on sale; mostly she window-shopped outside boutiques like "Soap Galore." Since the driver had promised to tell me when we got to Catron Street, I looked out the window with Lyn. At first the houses were exactly like ours— fake brick boxes with one picture window and a square of grass between the front steps and the sidewalk. We have a bird bath that I keep filled for the sparrows, but other people do different things with the space. Lyn poked me. "Look, Em, tall pink birds, look at Mother Goose and her babies." The kid loved that garbage.

As we neared Westfield, she was bored with the view. The houses were all different and stood back from the street behind a few trees and bushes.

"Catron Street, girls," the driver called and smiled at Lyn as we got off.

1105 was gray stucco with a pitched roof and pointed windows made of little leaded panes. The windows were dark. Two big blue spruce that looked as if they wanted to take over the world stood on either side of the front door and rattled in the wind.

"Why are we here?" Lyn whined.

"To sell raffle tickets, stupid." I rang the door bell.

"My teddy is cold."

It had started to rain, and she was shaking inside the red plastic coat. I rang the bell again. The door opened, and Mrs. Carter stood shivering in the wet wind. I knew it was Mrs. Carter because she was so beautiful. Blue eyes, blonde hair, the same as Lyn's.

"We're selling raffle tickets for St. John's. First prize is a color TV."

Mrs. Carter smiled a pearly smile, but looked bewildered. Part of "we" was invisible. I stepped aside. "This is Lyn." I shoved the kid forward.

"She's my sister," Lyn chirped.

Mrs. Carter stopped smiling. Her eyes turned into tiny blue points fixed on Lyn. For a moment I thought she was going to slam the door, but then a telephone rang somewhere in the shadows behind her.

"Come in out of the rain," she said, and we followed down a dark hall toward the back of the house. She was a small woman, and wore a pink shirt and designer jeans. My Mom would have called her too skinny because her shoulder blades showed under the shirt, but to me she looked terrific. At the end of the hall we came into a bright gleaming room, the kind of kitchen I'd seen in magazines, that doesn't look like a kitchen because all the stuff is hidden behind knotty pine or sunk in tiled islands. The glass doors in the wall at the far end were open. Beyond them was a jungle.

"Go sit down, girls, while I answer the phone." Mrs. Carter pointed to some white wicker furniture grouped around a ficus.

"Let's explore," I said to Lyn, and took her hand.

We walked along a narrow flagstone path bordered by flowering plants banked against tiers of taller foliage. When I was little, Dad used to take me to the Bronx Botanical Garden, so I recognized the ferns and some flowers in the dense steamy growth that filled the greenhouse.

"Cyclamen," I told Lyn, who was squishing along in her rubber boots as we passed terra-cotta pots and drift-wood and rocks and shells, all spilling out plants.

"Look," Lyn whispered.

Shorter than me, she was the first to see the frog hiding under a pink azalea. In fact, there were frogs everywhere—green ones with yellow polka dots, yellow with green polka dots, white china frogs with blue violets growing out of their backs, and tiny glass frogs squatting on the leaves of a high-climbing philodendron.

"Aren't they cute?" Mrs. Carter appeared from behind some tall plants with spiky leaves. She had a wispy voice that reminded me of Peter Lorre in *The Maltese Falcon*. "Every time Mr. Carter goes on a trip for his company, he brings me one."

"He must travel a lot," I said as she pointed to three frogs peeking out of a hanging basket above my head.

"Yes, but he loves to come home to this. It's his Garden of Eden." She hurried over to a wrought iron stand and rearranged some gloxinia around a color photograph. Mr. Carter looked kind of old. He also looked like a frog. "While he's away, his plants keep me company." She bent down and fingered the hairy leaves of a begonia. "Must check for mealy bugs. I'm in charge of pest control."

Apparently she didn't find any pests, but she took a list out of her jeans pocket, studied it for a minute, and then we went and sat down on the wicker chairs.

"My sister knows the names of all the state flowers," Lyn announced.

"Lyn can recite the Pledge of Allegiance. She's very smart for her age," I said, and waited, but the kid kept her eyes down like she'd never seen a floor.

Mrs. Carter sat on the edge of her chair and stared into the jungle. Suddenly she jumped up. "Must get rid of those aphids before Mr. Carter comes home."

She went into a shed at the side of the greenhouse, and I followed.

"Nicotine. Where's the nicotine spray?" she muttered as she rummaged among the bottles and cans on the floor under a shelf.

"I think it's there to your left, Mrs. Carter."

She grabbed the spray and, getting to her feet, looked me up and down with surprise. "Do you know about plants?"

"I worked in my uncle's flower shop last summer."

"Good, I need help. The perperomnia by the sink. Luke-warm water, soap, cotton swabs."

She hurried into the greenhouse, and I swabbed each leaf and stem carefully. Through the window of the shed I could see Mrs. Carter's pink shirt darting in and out of the green. Whenever she passed Lyn in the wicker chair, she stopped for a minute, told her about thrips and lice and scale and maggots and mites and fungi. Each time, Lyn curled up like a frightened caterpillar and held her teddy to her face. I felt sorry for her and kept hoping Mrs. Carter would explain that those bugs don't attack humans, but she was in too much of a rush.

Mrs. Carter really loved those plants. She knew what they liked to eat, and how much sun or shade they needed, and she talked to them, calling each one by name and encouraging it to fight the pests.

"I'll be there in a minute," she called to me. "Get out the six-inch pots. Make sure they're clean. No bacteria."

I found the pots and waited. The rain was bouncing off the glass roof like hail, but the air inside the greenhouse was warm and had a woodsy smell.

"Aren't you too hot in that coat?" Mrs. Carter asked Lyn, who sat sulking with her teddy.

"It's raining," Lyn mumbled, scrunching further inside the red plastic.

"Potting mixture. This bin," Mrs. Carter said, coming into the shed. She scooped the soil onto the wooden bench. "Roots, that's what potting is all about." She tapped the sides of a pot and lifted the plant out. "See how these roots, poor things, are hunting for food? Now follow me." She placed a pot containing a scrawny dud in front of me.

I once repotted a spider plant my Mom had growing in the picture window, but working alongside Mrs. Carter made me clumsy. I couldn't keep up with her, and I was terrified I might hurt the roots. She was already on her second pot while I struggled, but she didn't notice.

"I'll give you both a nice shady spot and tomorrow some chelate of iron for those yellow leaves," she said, and carried them into the greenhouse.

Once I was alone, I worked quickly, pressing the soil

firmly around the roots and keeping it level until it reached an inch below the rim so water wouldn't run off. Over the sound of the rain I could hear Lyn talking to Mrs. Carter.

"My teddy's name is Griff Junior after my daddy, and my mommy's going to bring me a new doll. I'll call her Emmie after my sister."

"You're a lucky girl to have such a wonderful sister."

Lyn nodded and made a face. "We don't have any frogs in our house. Griff Junior doesn't like frogs. He's afraid of them."

Mrs. Carter looked hurt and walked away. My plan to get rid of Lyn on her natural mother was in big trouble. I grabbed the plant and rushed out of the shed. "I hope this will be okay, Mrs. Carter."

She took off her gloves and tested the soil with her fingertips. She had beautiful long nails, polished silver. "Good, Em," she said, smiling at the plant.

"I need to go to the bathroom," Lyn whined.

"Come, it's just off the kitchen. And then we'll have a Coke."

I sat down and watched the rain, now a soft drizzle, streak the glass against the dark sky. The greenhouse was very peaceful. The plants, washed and sprayed for pests, filled the air with their breathing.

Mrs. Carter returned with the Cokes. Lyn jiggled the ice in her glass to get rid of the fizz, but fortunately she kept her trap shut. Mrs. Carter sat on the edge of her chair and stared into the jungle, watching for pests.

"Griff Junior wants to go home." Lyn's loud whisper jolted Mrs. Carter into motion.

"Must pinch back Lady Washington, Mr. Carter's favorite." Her long silver nails snipped the new green ends of a large geranium that hadn't yet bloomed. "As soon as I'm finished, I'll drive you home."

Lyn put on her rain hat and said, "Then you can see our house. I live at 209 Maple Street. The phone number is . . ."

My Mom had made her memorize our address and phone number in case she got lost.

"Mrs. Carter doesn't need your phone number, stupid," I whispered as I carried the Coke glasses into the kitchen.

I didn't want Mrs. Carter to see our tacky house with the spider plant in the picture window, but it was getting late, and if we weren't home by five, Aunt Ethel would call Detective Schmidt and the FBI.

Mrs. Carter drove slowly. Lyn had scrambled into the back seat, although there was plenty of room in the front of the Le Baron. At every red light Mrs. Carter looked in the mirror and squinted hard, first at Lyn and then at her own face.

"You can just leave us at the corner," I said, but the light was green. She made the turn and stopped in front of the house. The lantern with the yellow plastic panes over the front door was lit, but at least Aunt Ethel was not standing on the stoop in her floral print housecoat. Lyn got out of the car and ran into the house.

"Thanks for the ride, Mrs. Carter. I really liked working in the potting shed, and the frogs were fantastic."

"You're a good worker, Em." She opened her purse and handed me twelve dollars.

When I protested that it was too much, she said she didn't have change and anyway she liked having me around, because with Mr. Carter away she worried a lot about the greenhouse.

"Lyn and I both had a great time. I hope that plant I repotted will be okay."

"Adiantum, maidenhair fern. Needs shade and moisture."

Mrs. Carter had drifted back to the Garden of Eden, but when I opened the car door, she turned to me and said, "Maybe you'd like to come sometime and see how it's doing."

"I'll come tomorrow. Can I bring Lyn? She'll behave better when she gets used to you."

She leaned against the steering wheel and curled her fingers around it. "I don't think Lyn likes me any more than she likes my frogs. Maybe she'd rather stay home with her dolls."

"She can bring her dolls. One, anyway."

"I guess you can bring her if you want. She is your sister."

I was about to say, "No, she's not. Can't you see she's your kid?" But Mrs. Carter turned the key in the ignition and said, as I got out of the car, "Em, you should plant some chrysanthemums around that birdbath. Korean hybrids, hardy, disease resistant."

I went to Mrs. Carter's every afternoon for the rest of the week. Each time Lyn hassled me with, "I want to stay home. It's spooky there. The frog-lady's scary."

"You're a chicken liver," I hissed, which made her giggle.

"Can I bring Baby Emmie?"

That Cabbage Patch preemie is gross, but I said okay.

Each day I got better at repotting. Mrs. Carter said I was a natural when it came to plants. When I arrived, the first thing I did was check on the maidenhair fern. Mrs. Carter had placed it in a shaded area among other ferns and a few frogs. It looked lousy, the fronds limp and grayish. A read dud. Mrs. Carter said plants need time to recover from the shock of being transplanted. Not every one of them makes it. The pests attack, the roots don't take hold.

I had tons of work in the shed. Mrs. Carter tacked a list on the door, but by now I didn't need reminding to wash used pots, stack clean pots, prepare soil mixes. She noticed immediately that I had arranged the pesticides alphabetically and she thought that was a neat idea. I thought she was fantastic, kind of queer at times, like when she couldn't find certain frogs and told me they jumped from one spot to another at night to make her look for them. Whenever she moved plants around, I did my best to remember which frogs belonged where.

Each day Mrs. Carter got more hyper. She rushed from one project to the other and disappeared for long periods in the jungle. When Mom and Dad were around, they were right there, solid, bulky shapes with red faces, but Mrs. Carter was small and pale and moved so quickly, I was never sure where she was, and when she stood still, all I could see through the foliage was a patch of colored shirt and some blonde hair. I knew she was lonely even with all the plants to keep her company, because by the middle of the afternoon she would come to the shed and say, "You must be tired, Em. Let's have a Coke." I still had lots of things I wanted to do and I wasn't a bit tired, but I could see that she was, so I tidied up the benches, cleaned the sink, put away the bone meal, chelate of iron, peat moss, humus, and all my other stuff.

At Coke time Lyn was a real nuisance. She squeezed into my chair, and whenever Mrs. Carter spoke to me,

Lyn interrupted with, "Em, look at my sore finger. Em, fix my coat collar." Sun streamed into the greenhouse, but she wore the red raincoat anyway.

"Maybe she would like to watch TV," Mrs. Carter suggested one afternoon. "There's a TV in the breakfast alcove."

"Baby Emmie loves Mister Rogers," Lyn said, and kept calling, "Em, come see. He's in color."

We don't have color, and the next day was Saturday, so Lyn was looking forward to all those dumb cartoons and didn't bug me.

"Mrs. Carter likes you a lot," I told her, once we were on the bus.

"She likes you better."

"If you took off that raincoat and looked at the plants once in a while, I'll bet she'd want you to stay with her for good and let you watch TV all you want."

"Don't wake the baby," Lyn whispered.

"When we get to Catron Street," I told her, "I'm going to ask Mrs. Carter about your staying with her the minute I get the chance." I rang the bell.

"She likes you best," Lyn whined as the door opened.

Mr. Carter, in a green jogging suit, filled the doorway.

"You must be the potting expert," he boomed. With his shiny forehead and wrinkled neck, he looked just like his picture, only older. "And so this is Lyn." He peered down. "What's that thing, Lyn?"

"It's just a preemie doll, Mr. Carter," I answered.

Once in the house, Lyn made for the TV, and I followed Mr. Carter into the greenhouse. He went down the path to see his Lady Washington, and I hurried over to my dud fern.

"Roots are taking hold," Mrs. Carter called to me from the crotons.

A gold charm dangled on a chain around her neck, a frog with jade eyes, a new present from Mr. Carter.

I checked the soil around the maidenhair. It was moist, but even if the roots were okay, the rest of the plant looked pretty sick. I went to work in the shed. Mr. Carter dashed in with a hanging basket under each arm. Being so tall, he could reach the fuchsias without a ladder.

Mr. Carter was a noisemaker. Humming old Sinatra songs and cussing himself and his tools, he filled the greenhouse with sound as he worked his way among the flowers like a gigantic bumblebee. He kept losing his tools, and then would shout, "Hon, I can't find the God-damned dibble." Mrs. Carter would rush to help him look for it. She was very lovey-dovey with him. He wanted to extend the God-damned greenhouse and maybe grow orchids. She held onto his hand and nodded, "Yes, dear."

As they walked along the flagstone path, she looked frail, tired. I didn't see how she could take on any more plants. There was no Coke that afternoon. With Mr. Carter home, Mrs. Carter took no time off. I didn't care, because I had so much to do, and with the next day being Sunday and Aunt Ethel insisting on church, I wanted to finish repotting the fuchsias so Mr. Carter could hang them. Around four o'clock Lyn wandered into the shed. "We want to go home," she said.

I was sure she would knock over my pots or get poisoned from all the "Keep out of Reach of Children" powders and sprays.

"Go sit down and play. I'll be ready soon."

"When is soon?"

"In a minute. Baby Emmie could get sick in here."

She covered the doll's face with its pink blanket and

ran out to the wicker chair. The next time I looked up from my bench, she had spread the doll's clothes on the table and was changing diapers.

"Hon, I can't find my grafting knife," Mr. Carter shouted from the back of the greenhouse. Mrs. Carter must have gone into the house because there was no answer, and Mr. Carter kept muttering "stupid fool" to himself and cursing the knife for getting lost. "You in the kitchen, Hon?" he called. Then I heard a bellow and looked up to see him standing beside Lyn.

"Little girl, this is not a toy." He grabbed the knife from a corner of the table where he must have left it, and shook it at her.

I could see he was more worried-angry than angry, but Lyn couldn't handle it. She turned from white to pink, blinked, sucked in her lower lip, and, clutching Baby Emmie, dove under the table.

"You could lose a finger," Mr. Carter yelled through the wicker tabletop, and then went back into his Garden of Eden.

"The man doesn't like me," Lyn whimpered on the bus ride home.

"It's that weirdo doll," I said, but it was clear that Mr. Carter did not know as much about kids as he did about plants.

On Monday Lyn refused to come with me, even though I promised her Mr. Carter would be at work in his office or on a trip.

"Lyn's got a sore throat," I told Mrs. Carter when I arrived. She was in a hurry to show me something in the greenhouse. "See, Em," she pointed to little shoots that struggled up from the crown of the maidenhair. They looked so fragile, I wanted to do something immediately to help them, give them food or water. Mrs. Carter said to leave the plant alone.

The Garden of Eden was very quiet without Mr. Carter. Since Saturday a lot of things had been moved. Gigantic urns of Lady Washington had been placed near the wicker furniture and the ficus now stood in filtered light in a corner. Pots of yellow and red kalanchoe surrounded the wooden tub, no trace of fungi on their thick, fleshy leaves.

"The place looks great," I said. "You must have worked all day yesterday."

Mrs. Carter sighed and began walking along the path. She was wearing a purple shirt. The color dulled the blue of her eyes and she seemed spaced out.

"Mr. Carter likes to keep busy," she said so quietly I could barely hear her. "He didn't mean to scare Lyn."

"She wasn't scared. She wanted to come, but Aunt Ethel kept her home."

"Make cuttings," Mrs. Carter told herself, and took a list out of her jeans. "Begonias today."

I left her talking to a Rex begonia and went into the shed. Trays of sand had been spread on the benches. On the counter next to the sink lay several legal-sized pages stamped DON'T FORGET in red letters. Tiny handwriting covered the pages.

"Cheesecloth, Em," Mrs. Carter said, rushing into the shed carrying the Rex begonia. "Mr. Carter just phoned to remind me. We need it to protect the cuttings. Where did I put it?"

I found the cheesecloth in a drawer.

"Thanks, Em. Such a help." She brushed her hair back off her face and handed me a knife.

I had seen a slide show about propagation at the

Botanical Garden. It was strange how a leaf or stem that had no roots went ahead and made roots after being cut off the plant. Taking cuttings looked easy in the slides. Mrs. Carter clipped a large leaf off the Rex begonia and put it in the tray in front of me.

Her gloved hands snipped, cut, pressed. "Don't let leaves touch each other or they rot. Sand warm and moist," she said. I stared at the blotched leaf on my tray. The stalk looked watery and was covered with hairs. With the knife I flipped the leaf over. Reddish veins crisscrossed the underside. I knew I was supposed to slice into the main vein, but I couldn't. The thought of that oozing wound and a new plant growing out of it was too gross. Mrs. Carter didn't notice as I left the shed.

"Cokes here on the table," she called when I came out of the bathroom. "Begonias finished."

I didn't feel much like a Coke, but to be polite I sat down beside her.

"Pelargoniums, gloxinias tomorrow," she read off her list. "Lots to do, but we can finish by Friday, Em."

I held the cold glass with both hands. "Mrs. Carter, I'm not sure I can come. My parents get home from Syracuse and I ought to . . . "

"Remind me, Em, charcoal dust. It prevents damping off."

"School starts next week. If I don't do better, Miss Watts could make me repeat the year. She told my Mom that I wasn't working to my full potential. That's teacher talk for goofing off."

I hated talking about school. All vacation while working for Mrs. Carter, I had shoved the thought of Miss Watts out of my head.

"Lyn thinks you're best in the class." In Mrs. Carter's Peter Lorre voice it sounded like a question.

"I tell Lyn a lot of nutty stuff. Makes her feel important. You know, playing the big sister."

Mrs. Carter leaned on the arm of her chair and stopped watching the Garden of Eden grow. "You don't like Lyn, do you?" she asked, facing me.

For me to lie to her would have been like using a dirty pot, and besides, I needed to get rid of that scab that had been growing inside me like the horrible scale she was always spraying.

"I don't like her much." Saying it felt good. "Anyway, we're not really sisters."

"I know. She told me."

"She did?"

"Yes. She told me you're adopted."

I felt suddenly cut off from myself, unable to breathe and shout that I wasn't, that Lyn was a liar.

Mrs. Carter's voice came and went in whispers. "People are like plants. Roots, soil . . ."

Her words drifted, and finally I couldn't hear or see her. Enormous ferns swayed above my head, and in their shadow the air was thick with fumes of fertilizer and pesticides. I tried to escape to the potting shed, but the path had disappeared under overgrown babies' tears and phlox. The shed floated out of sight in a green mist.

"Lyn's looking for you." Mrs. Carter peeked out from a clump of bamboo. Her pale face blurred into Mr. Carter's big frog smile. "You're a natural, Em. Need you to repot this God-damned fuchsia," he bawled.

Lyn was crying for me from under the table.

"Help us, help us," Mrs. Carter echoed Mr. Carter.

"Leave me alone," I yelled back, fighting off the vines

trailing orange and purple fuchsia blossoms. "I can't help everyone. You're both loonies."

I leaned over to pick up Lyn. "Don't worry, Em," I heard Mrs. Carter say. The ice rattled in my glass as she touched my arm. "She will be all right, but even with a good home she needs lots of care to help her grow."

I took a deep breath. "My Mom and Dad spoil her rotten. They're super-great to both of us, but she sucks up to them so they baby her. She's not a baby."

Mrs. Carter nodded, sipping her Coke. "No, she's old enough to feel frightened, afraid of getting lost." She waved her hand. "Imagine, getting lost here in that red raincoat."

"That's dumb."

"Maybe. She's not very strong."

"Then she's a dud."

"Needs lots of attention," Mrs. Carter sighed and went back to studying her "Don't forget" sheet. "Primulas next week. You'll be in school."

I didn't listen as she read the list. Lyn was a dud. The idea blew my mind. I still didn't like her much, especially since she had screwed up with Mrs. Carter, but now the thought of school and Miss Watts was taking so much hate energy, I didn't have any left over for Lyn.

"Em, you could take a couple of primulas home. They like a cool, airy room, indirect light."

I explained that Aunt Ethel was making meatloaf for supper. The night before my Dad gets home, she always makes "her" meatloaf for him. He eats it cold in sandwiches on rye bread with ketchup. The primulas wouldn't like a house that heats up when the oven is on and every room stinks of garlic and tomato sauce.

"Four-inch pots, Em," Mrs. Carter said.

138

"Hello, Hon, hello, Emeline. Home early." Mr. Carter bounded into the greenhouse. Mrs. Carter jumped up and went over to him. "We finished the begonia cuttings."

"Great. Jerry's here. I need help with that ventilator."

Jerry appeared from the kitchen, a tall, skinny guy in sweat pants and a black jacket with red satin devils on the front pockets.

"My stepson Jerry. Jerry, this is Emeline," Mrs. Carter said.

We shook hands and then backed off.

"Come on, Jer. Over here in the south corner." Mr. Carter led the way. Jer shrugged and followed. Across the back of his jacket "Demons" was stitched in red letters.

"It's getting late. I have to go," I told Mrs. Carter. "You needn't pay me for this afternoon. I didn't do anything."

Suddenly the greenhouse echoed with sounds of coughing and sneezing.

"Kid's still got that God-damned allergy," Mr. Carter said, coming out of the Garden of Eden.

"Can he give Em a lift on his way home?" Mrs. Carter asked.

"Sure. Give Em a lift, Jer," Mr. Carter yelled over his shoulder and then headed for the potting shed to check on the cuttings.

Jerry took his face out of his handkerchief, nodded, and when we got outside, leaned against the hood of a yellow VW bug. He was still choking for breath.

"You okay?" I asked, worried about his driving.

"In a minute. Get in."

When I opened the door, I noticed the side of the

car was plastered with decals, nothing but small red devils.

"Hope I'm not too far out of your way," I said as he wound himself into the driver's seat.

"No sweat. Maple is near where I live."

"You're on your own?"

"Yeah. The family of a friend of mine, he's on the team, lets me live over their garage. It's okay when they're away. Then I can use the kitchen in the house. The rest of the time I have to eat out. Lots of Lota Burgers."

"We're having meatloaf tonight at my house. Aunt Ethel always makes tons, and there'd be plenty for you if you don't hate meatloaf with garlic and tomato."

"Thanks a lot, but I have a date shooting baskets with some of the guys. Maybe another time."

At rush hour the crosstown traffic moved slowly. He kept cutting in and out of the left lane like he was Mario Andretti.

"I'm not in a hurry," I said. "What happened to your tape deck?" There was a hole under the dash.

"I forgot to lock the car while I was at the game last night."

There was an opening in the right lane and he went for it.

"Are you on the team?"

"Not tall enough. Those guys are skyscrapers. Anyway, my timing is lousy."

"You're a good driver, though. If we stay in this lane, lots of cars turn off for the parkway."

"Yeah, might as well stay in line with the lemmings. The Demons have a great team this year. Would you like to go to a game sometime? I could pick you up."

"Sure."

"Don't expect the Celtics, but we all have a blast."

A trailer truck slowed in front of us, and the VW wheezed as if it wanted to quit.

"It must have your allergy. I'm allergic too. Ragweed and goldenrod destroy me."

"I'm not allergic." He gunned the motor, and we zoomed around the truck. "I just get this asthma every time I go to Catron Street."

"Could be the pesticides."

"It's my Dad and his fucking Garden of Eden. That's why I moved out."

He started coughing again and had to wipe his eyes on the sleeve of his jacket.

"Red light ahead," I warned.

The VW shuddered to a stop.

"And those frogs. I hate the whole scene."

I believed him. Hate was pouring out of him, I could feel the heat of it reddening his eyes and nose. Even the lobes of his ears were pink under his hair. He stiff-armed the steering wheel and pounded on it. A woman in the next car stared at us.

"Light's changed," I said and inched against the door on my side.

"The way he calls me Jer, like we're buddies." He shifted into first, and the VW lurched forward. " 'Jer, help with the ventilator.' 'Jer, give me a hand with this trellis.' What a bunch of garbage!"

To get off his problems with his father, I said, "Mrs. Carter is a terrific lady. I learned a lot working for her."

He slammed on the brakes and said, "She's pathetic."

Cars, blocked behind us, were honking. Some drivers

passed. One in a pickup yelled, "Learn to drive, kid!" I got out.

"See you next Demons' home game," Jerry called as I ran to the sidewalk.

A minute later the VW passed me. He beeped and waved. I kept on running.

"Lyn and I were worried," Aunt Ethel said when I reached the stoop. She gave me a garlicky kiss. "You must have sold all those raffle tickets by now."

I suddenly felt a lump in my jeans pocket. Mrs. Carter had kept me so busy, I had forgotten about the tickets.

The next morning, right after breakfast, I took off for Catron Street. Mrs. Carter opened the door. The pockets of her gardening apron sagged with the weight of tools.

"Oh, Em, I am glad to see you. Red spider mites on the cineraria." She stepped aside to let me in.

"I've come about the raffle tickets," I said, not moving from the front step.

"Raffle tickets?"

"For the church bazaar. They are ten dollars a book, and if you don't buy some, I'll be in big trouble when my Mom gets home tonight."

"Come in. My purse is in the kitchen."

As we walked down the hall, she said, "Last night Jerry had to come back for some of his things. That boy has such awful allergies, he'll never make the team, which is all he thinks about. Maybe you can help him, convince him to see a doctor. He likes you. He won't listen to his father or me. Now where did I leave my purse?"

"There by the phone."

She took three tens out of her wallet. I gave her the tickets to fill in her name and address, so that if she won something, the bazaar ladies could reach her.

"I'll do that later, Em." She took the tickets. "Go

take a look at your fern and then meet me in the shed. I'm way behind with the gloxinia cuttings."

From the kitchen I watched her hurry across the flagstones. She stopped for a moment by the wicker furniture to examine the Lady Washingtons. They were in full sunlight, and the pale pink blossoms were just opening. She whispered something about gray mold and went into the shed. I followed her, but she was working so furiously over the sand trays that she didn't notice me standing in the doorway until I said, "Thanks for buying the tickets. If you give me the stubs, I'll fill them in for you."

She put down the knife and looked up.

"Did you check the maidenhair?"

"No, I've got to hurry. Aunt Ethel wants me to clean the mess in my room before school starts, and I promised to help Lyn organize her doll house. She likes things neat."

"How's Lyn's throat?"

"Okay. She is a very healthy kid."

Mrs. Carter crouched down and groped around under the bench. I stepped forward to help her, but she said, "Never mind, Em, I can manage. They're hiding, but I'll find them. Here we are." She stood up and put the primulas in a shopping bag. "When you get home, remember, cool temperature, indirect light, watch for leaf spot."

"Maybe if I get my marks up, I can help you some afternoons."

"I'm always here, Em." She picked up the cutting knife.

"Good morning, Miss Emeline. Good girl, early on the job. I'm late. Here's the list, Hon."

Mr. Carter, dressed in a blue business suit, tore into

the shed. I squeezed myself and the shopping bag past him and out the doorway. When I reached the kitchen, I looked back. He took the raffle tickets from Mrs. Carter and said, "I'll mail them. Maybe I can get home early tonight."

"That would be a help, Hon." She smiled up at him.

He put his arm around her shoulders. When I left, they were standing side by side, steadying each other and hanging on with all their strength.

At home I put the primulas on the dresser in my room and opened the window.

"What are those?" Lyn asked, stepping around a pile of T-shirts and socks.

"Plants, stupid. Don't touch. They've just been transplanted and their roots are delicate."

"No frogs," she said, and left the room.

The primulas lasted ten days. While I was at school, Mom closed the window and the room got hot and dry. When I opened it, I couldn't study on account of the cold. The blossoms withered and leaf spot took over. The plants had to go in the trash, but I saved the pots, scrubbed them, and kept them on the dresser.

One day, when I came home from school, my Mom called from the kitchen, "Somebody named Jerry phoned." She stopped chopping onions for potato salad and took an old envelope with a number scribbled on it from her apron pocket. "He wants you to go to a basketball game. Who is this boy Jerry?"

"Just a guy I met."

She wiped her hands on a wet dishrag and looked at me hard. Her eyes were watering from the onions. "Well, you can tell me who he is later, but for now you shouldn't go out with him. From the sound of him he's got a terrible cold."

"He's allergic to his father."

"Poor boy. Hand me the mayo, Em dear."

The only phone in our house is on the wall next to the kitchen sink, so while talking to Jerry I had to keep ducking out of my Mom's way. He sounded a lot better than that time in the VW.

"The Demons are on a roll. It'll be a great game tonight. Want to come?"

I explained that I had to study every minute because of final exams and horrible Miss Watts.

"That bitch still on your back?"

"She's in shock. I got a B-minus in American History, but math is a real sweat. It's my worst subject, and my Dad will be really upset if I fail."

"Sounds like a bummer."

"I don't want to let him down by not studying. I'll probably fail anyway."

"Are you in the shower?"

"My Mom's washing stuff in the kitchen sink. Maybe we could go to a game when school's over."

Jerry said okay, and I said how much I wanted to see the Demons play and meet all his friends. Then we hung up.

After that, all I did was worry and study. Some afternoons, when I couldn't concentrate any longer, I stared out my bedroom window and watched the sparrows fight around the birdbath. Since I was so busy, I told Lyn to keep it clean and filled with water, then maybe the pink birds with the long legs would come and drink. The grass was full of dandelions, but seen from above they looked pretty. I thought of Mrs. Carter walking along borders of primulas. Behind them tulips and hyacinths would be blooming like crazy. She would take good care of my fern, but I missed seeing it, and the empty pots on the dresser reminded me of leaf mold and all the other blights that attacked her plants in the Garden of Eden.

My Dad made up math problems for me every evening after supper, the sort of equations most likely to be on the exam, and instead of going bowling or watching TV, he went over my answers. The night before the exam he put his arm around me and said, "Don't worry. You're trying. That counts more than grades with your Mom and me." I went to bed and felt worse than the time when I overheard him say to my Mom, "We always have Em."

The exam was a real stinker, and I was the last in the class to turn in my blue book. I caught the last bus home, and when I got off, I saw Jerry's yellow VW parked in front of the house. It had lost the front left fender, and something had scraped a couple of devils off the door.

"Hi," Jerry said from the driver's seat. "You look beat." He kicked open the door, and I sat down next to him. The floor was littered with empty cans and Lota Burger cartons.

"How'd the exam go?"

"I don't want to talk about it. I'll know on Friday. What happened to your car?"

"Some nerd banged into it in the parking lot while I was at last week's game. The Demons are playing tonight. Want to go?"

"I'll have to ask my parents. My Dad was talking about taking us out to the Steak House for supper now that I've finished all my exams."

"My Dad has really lost his marbles. Guess what's next in the Garden of Eden."

I didn't want to hear about his father, but Jerry didn't wait for me to guess.

"Get this. He's going to grow Tokay grapes."

Secretly I liked the idea of Mr. Carter with his long arms training the vines on a trellis. Plucking a God-damned grape, he would hand it to Mrs. Carter, who would take it in her silvery fingertips and place the Tokay between her teeth.

"Perfect, Hon. Very sweet," she would say and reach up to hold his hand.

"Grapes," Jerry gasped and kicked at an empty can under his feet.

I waited for him to catch his breath and then I said, "Mrs. Carter wants me to work for her this summer."

"You'd be a fool, breaking your ass for her in the potting shed."

"I'm starting as soon as school is out."

The tip of his nose turned red, and he began to cough.

"You're as weird as she is," he shouted after me as I got out of the VW and ran to the house.

My Mom was waiting at the door. "Come have some iced tea, dear. You must be tired."

I followed her into the kitchen. For once it was cool, nothing stewing on top of the stove.

"Jerry's still got that cold," she said, opening the fridge. "With the window open, I could hear him coughing."

"It's not a cold," I said to her back. "Have you got any limes?"

"Yes, and fresh mint. Run this under the tap." She turned and handed me the ice tray. "What's the matter with Jerry if it's not a cold?"

"He's a dud."

"That's a harsh, ugly word, Em dear." She reminded me that we all had faults.

Like I said, my parents are very loving, and I was beginning to see that Lyn and Mr. and Mrs. Carter were all duds in their way, but Jerry was a special case.

"Mom, he's a self-made dud full of hate."

The tray, furry with frost, burned in my hand. As I dropped it in the sink, I noticed, on the window ledge above the sink, a pot with a large white azalea. I recognized it immediately.

"Isn't that lovely?" Mom said and stood beside me. "A present from your friend, Mrs. Carter. Go sit down. I'll get the ice."

I sat at the kitchen table and stared at the plant while she told me that Mrs. Carter had won an electric broom in the raffle.

"Your father and I decided to drive to Catron Street today during his lunch hour and deliver it. He wanted to meet her, and since you are going to be working there this summer, I needed to see the place and make sure she is the right sort of person."

"Did you take Lyn?"

"No, just the electric broom. Lyn calls her scary. Mrs. Carter *is* a little strange, but she's very kind, and your father got a big kick out of the frogs. She said you would know how to take care of the plant."

"Acid soil, watch for lace bug and white fly."

She glanced at the azalea. "Just what she said. Mrs. Carter is very fond of you. You're her favorite. We had a nice talk."

"Did you talk about Lyn?"

"Your father did, about how we've adopted her and love her as if she were our own. Drink your tea, Em, before all the ice melts. In this warm weather the re-frigerator takes forever to make more."

"Lyn and Mrs. Carter look a lot alike."

"Yes, they do, but my goodness that woman is a worrier. While she was showing us the greenhouse, she went on and on about people and plants. You know the way she talks, this soil, that light. Don't you think she worries too much?"

I agreed that Mrs. Carter worried a lot.

"Not good around children. To her, every sniffle would mean pneumonia. Maybe that's the problem with Jerry."

"Come on, Mom. A child doesn't have a driver's license and own a car." I sipped the tea and thought how great she was with me and all my allergies.

"Anyway, Mrs. Carter and your father and I agreed that a greenhouse with all those terrible pests is no place for a six-year-old. Then she gave me the azalea, and we left."

"So I shouldn't take Lyn with me anymore?"

"No. She is counting on your help. She doesn't want Lyn. Now go put on a dress so we don't keep your father waiting."

When I arrived at school Friday morning, I was told to go to Miss Watts' office. She was on the phone, so I slumped into the chair by her desk and turned my mind off by staring at a couple of African violets on the windowsill behind her. The pink one looked okay, but the white had probs. I suspected leaf spot. When she hung up and leaned across the desk, her shoulder blocked out the white violet, so I focused on the pink.

"Emeline, I am satisfied you can do the work. The B on the math exam helped your average. Maybe the situation at home this past year, a new member of the family, was too much of a distraction for you."

I tuned out the rest of the stuff about how great I could do next year if I applied myself and developed good work habits. Finally her lips stopped moving and after a pause I heard her ask, "Emeline, you're not listening. Is there something going on outside my window?" She spun around in her chair and put her glasses on.

"It's your African violet, Miss Watts, the white one."

She removed her glasses and peered at the plant.

"Maybe it's got leaf spot," I said.

"Mr. Thomas in botany gave me that," she said, as if it was contagious.

I told her not to wet the leaves when watering and to spray with a fungicide. As I ducked out the door, she was writing "bordeaux mixture" on her calendar.

Saturday morning, while I was working on my hair with my Mom's blow dryer, Lyn came into the bathroom carrying Emmie number six, the one from Syracuse. Except for the preemie who was squashed and bald, it looked like all the others, dimples, curls. During exam week my Dad had warned Lyn not to pester me. Now she watched as if she'd never seen hair before, and when I turned off the dryer to plaster some more mousse on the cowlick, she asked, "Who's Arthur?"

"My Uncle Arthur, stupid. He's married to my Mom's sister in Boston."

Lyn sat down on the john. "I'm not stupid. You're stupid. I mean the Arthur who's coming to stay with us."

Lyn is a terrific snoop. She's got listening devices implanted under that fluff, but she often plays things back wrong. As soon as my Mom came home from K Mart, I ran into the kitchen and asked her what was going on.

"Little Arthur, your cousin. How nice your hair looks, Em, now that you're taking care of it. Help me with these packages."

"Pampers. Why did you buy a ton of Pampers?"

"He's only six months. Aunt Helen is very sick, so he'll be staying with us."

"Told you so," Lyn whispered.

"How sick is she?"

"Very. I'm going to Boston tomorrow to get the baby, and I want you two girls to work together and look after your father. I'll leave a chicken casserole on the stove."

Lyn began to wail about Mommy's leaving her.

"No more of that any more, Lyn. Put these in the closet. When I come home, you can help take care of your cousin Arthur."

After Lyn put the Pampers away, we went out and sat on the stoop.

"We're here. Why does Arthur have to come here?" she asked.

"It's our Mom. She's got a thing about little babies."

"Stop your crying." Lyn gave Emmie number six a shake.

I keep wads of Kleenex in my jeans pocket in case the pollen count rises. I took one out. "Here's for both of you."

Lyn wiped her eyes, and we went in for lunch.